Who w

Paradox

The Angels Are here

Book 1

Patti Roberts

REVIEWS

Patti Roberts writes clearly and evokes an emotional reaction as well as deep thought in her readers, clearly an amazing writer. The reader will look forward to the sequel of this novel.
Krystal Larson – Book Reviewer

I wasn't supposed to read this book until I finished two others I had in front of it. After a peak inside I was sucked in and finished the book in one evening.
Julia Crane – Author

Having read Paradox – The Angels Are Here, I feel I've been left with a different world view on angels, heaven and spirituality.
Jayde Scott – Author

Patti Roberts has a powerful way of putting you in the story.
Lenore Wolfe - Author

Paradox Promotions
Covers & Formatting
http://bit.ly/paradoxcovers

Copyright © 2011 Patti Roberts

Edited By Ella Medler &
Tabitha Ormiston- Smith
Blog: http://paradoxangels.blogspot.com.au/

ISBN-13: 978-1463519780

ASIN: B004QTOQQ

Paradox

Grigori – The original vampires.

Bulguardi – guardian angels.

"Paradox — the ephemeral link between what was and what could be, the legends of two worlds fused into one lethally warped reality."

Ella Medler, Paper Gold Publishing.

Since the Time Before Time, angelic races, good and evil, have existed. Unseen by the untrained eye, they moved silently through creation.

In an ancient kingdom, the battle between good and evil ensued, and within time, the battle lines expanded into new frontiers - a New World called Earth.

When the first angels fell, the original vampires, they quickly establish positions in the New World. The humans, unaware of the existence of these bloodthirsty beings, had no inclination that their world was about to change forever. Renowned for being the hunter, the human race quickly became the hunted.

As the vampires dominance spread throughout the world, threatening to engulf all humanity, a race of guardian angels soon followed, not only to protect their own from harm's way but to ensure the survival of the human race.

A young girl, Grace Connors, who unknowingly held the past and the future in the palm of her hand, had no idea of the role she was about to play in saving the human race.

In this riveting series, Patti Roberts sets in motion a sweeping time-travel fantasy originating in an ancient kingdom light years away. In a kingdom where supernatural forces, Gods, and magic reign, an elaborate tale of mythical creatures and unlikely heroes unfolds.

DEDICATION

For Audrey Dunn, my mum, who is walking with

The Angels – without her walking stick.

Forever in my heart.

RIP

And for all those that have ever endured the pain of a

broken heart. This is for you

CONTENTS

THE DEFINITION OF PARADOX

A seemingly illogical or self-contradictory
statement
or suggestion, that may in fact, be very true.

***

If life seems to have more questions than answers,
try to be the one who asks the questions.
Written by Charles Schulz

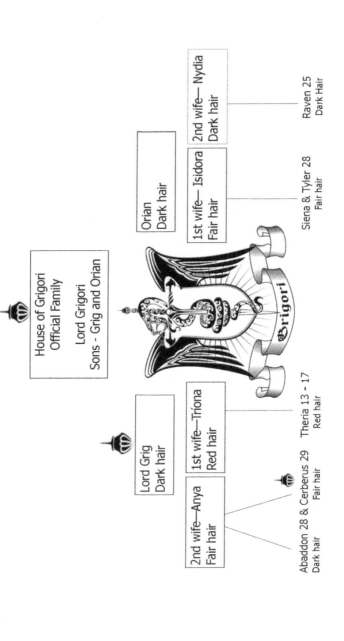

House of Grigori
Official Family

Lord Grigori
Sons - Grig and Orian

Orian
Dark hair

1st wife— Isidora
Fair hair

2nd wife— Nydia
Dark hair

Siena & Tyler 28
Fair hair

Raven 25
Dark Hair

Lord Grig
Dark hair

2nd wife—Anya
Fair hair

1st wife—Tríona
Red hair

Abaddon 28 & Cerberus 29
Dark hair   Fair hair

Theria 13 - 17
Red hair

Ancient World

Our souls are constructed from the very fabric of the universe – and have existed since the beginning of time.

The Ancients.

Thousands of years ago the world was a different place. One thing, however, regardless of the passing time and unimaginable distances that separate us remains unchanged. And that is–Love.

This chronicle tells a story that stretches out over a vast passage of time before spoken language was a necessity for communication. A time when magic existed and myths, legends, and the gods roamed the planets and walked freely among us all. It was a time long before the great floods consumed the Earth, before the Tower of Babel, or the stairway to the Gates of Heaven existed. The passage of time on Earth determined by observing the sun, the moon, the stars, and the rise and fall of the great oceans.

Human age was not determined by numbers, but rather by one's wisdom and knowledge. The lines drawn in the palm of the hand prophesied the soul's age, not the lines etched on the human face.

When the immortal soul had come to the end of its human experience, that passage of time — age being irrelevant — was determined by a force of pure energy. Some have called this energy force — God. At this time, the Angel of Death would reveal herself and save your soul.

For billions of years, every living thing resonated as one. Then everything changed. War and greed will do that. It changes everything. And by the end of the first Great War eons past, ancient texts, along with immeasurable knowledge, were destroyed, leaving humanity damaged and adrift.

But know this without any doubt, you are not alone in this ultimate struggle for survival. None of us, however, are immune to death, and just as spring follows winter, new life follows death.

1 – THE FALL

The Imperial City Of Altair - Aquila
Year: 1080 AD
The Ancient World

The sickly stench of death curled silently through majestic arched windows and coagulated, forming a thick gray cloud of wretchedness.

Burning torches hung randomly along high stone walls, illuminating the deserted Royal Palace. Stray swirls of smoke danced gracefully around elaborate marble columns that lined a black aisle. At the end of the aisle was an elevated dais that had formerly held four golden thrones.

Behind the one remaining throne hung a massive shield emblazoned with a serpent entwined on a gem-encrusted dagger. A masterpiece in bronze depicting the Grigorian Coat of Arms.

The remainder of the chamber was now devoid of the lavish furnishings that had once seated royalty in the Imperial City of Altair.

A lone male figure, eclipsed by the overwhelming size of the chamber, glared at the deserted throne as he paced. He waited - something he did not like to do - for the imminent arrival of the others.

His impatience was evident in every knotted muscle on his chiseled face. Raised black veins pulsed on his muscular throat, hands clenched by his sides. His eyes were yellow, like cat's eyes, with minuscule black specks for pupils. They transcended pure evil.

The long dark cape that he wore swept the floor behind him as he glided, ghostlike, across the marble surface. He walked over to a tall arched window and stopped, folding his arms across his broad chest.

His white open-necked shirt displayed a segment of a black inked serpent. It quivered across his chest as though alive. The remainder of the serpent, hidden by clothing, encircled his torso before continuing its rippling passage down his arm. The fanged head revealed itself from beneath the ruffled shirt cuff on his left wrist. Crimson blood dripped from one of the razor-sharp fangs. Human blood.

He looked out into the black night and watched as the city below continued to burn out of control. High on The Mountain of Seven the illuminated dome, centerpiece of the Pinnacle Sanctuary, was slowly starting to fade. Only flames from the fire cast light on the towering stone enclosure that safeguarded the crystal-domed structure.

Soon, the dome would be in complete darkness, he thought confidently, smiling to himself. He stood rigidly, conceited in his arrogance. His body, the immortal body of a perfect twenty-eight-year-old man, flexed with desire.

He felt indestructible and drunk on his self-love.

The Imperial City all but deserted after another day of fighting, lay broken, burnt and twisted below.

Once lined with the most exquisite architecture in the Aquila Constellation, the city stood darkened and scarred by the fires that continued to burn into the night. Ornate fountains and statues in the Gardens of Tranquility were now piles of rubble on the scorched ground.

With nothing spared, only rubble and ashy remains lay littered and smoldering across the ground. Embers floated in the smoky air, carried by random gusts of wind. Beauty no longer represented in the burnt remains of the Imperial City.

A small hooded figure darted vigilantly over the rubble, searching for signs of life among the torn and bloodied bodies. Her sorrowful quest was swiftly becoming a fruitless one.

Soaring flames roared into the night sky, lighting her way, as they licked, teased and devoured the remainder of the Imperial City, home of the Seven Pinnacles, Keepers of Mortal Souls.

Thousands of souls had already perished during the ninety-nine days of war. Thousands more would perish during this battle fought between good and evil. The war would rage on between the two most powerful houses of the Imperial City until only one remained: The House of the Bulguardians, Royal Guard of The Imperial City, or the rebellious House of Fallen Angels - the Grigorians.

The Grigorians, following the expulsion of their elders from the city by the Royal Imperial Guardians, were forced to flee Empyrean. Now, after centuries spent underground, the Grigorian were thirsty for revenge—at any cost.

During the March equinox, under the dark cover of night, the Grigorians rose silently from the depths of their cavernous lair, attacking the Royal Palace as it slept.

About time, Abaddon thought angrily, as he turned swiftly toward the towering arched entrance.

Seconds later, a female stood regally in the stone entry. "Abaddon?" the exquisite woman queried as she entered the great chamber, hands clasped at her waist.

His expression was unsettling as she advanced cautiously toward him, her tight, deep purple gown almost hidden by the long black cape that trailed behind her. Her fair hair, beautifully adorned with gemstones, was entwined in a continuous braid crowning her head. Her catlike eyes, a mirror image of his, were traits of the Grigorian bloodline.

Abaddon's arms remained folded across his inflated chest. "Cousin, where are the others, your sister, your brother?" he demanded.

"They are… they have other things on their mind, they will be ready when the time comes, I can assure you," she replied, pausing at a safe distance from him. She knew he could read her mind, all their minds if he chose to, with direct eye contact. Without direct eye contact, however, he could only sense their presence, not their thoughts. Nor was his violent temper any secret. She had been a victim of it herself on many occasions.

"Oh, I'm sure I can imagine what they have on their minds," he said, circling her.

"Your attendance here, however, is a testament to your commitment to the cause, Siena." A sly smile crossed his lips. He liked knowing that she feared him. He reveled in being feared. It made him feel more powerful, superior.

His slit eyes flashed to the entrance as he sensed another's imminent arrival. He turned in greeting as a girl, his younger sibling entered the smoky room and ran toward him.

"Ah, little sister, how divine you look, my child." He swung her up into his arms as a groom would a new bride, and kissed her hard on the mouth. She did not resist; he knew she welcomed it.

"Abaddon," Theria chirped through smiling, rose-colored lips, running her fingers through his dark hair. "Always an absolute pleasure, of course. Now, please put me down… And… I am *not,* a child!"

Abaddon laughed and released Theria to the marble floor, running his hand down her flowing, red hair. "You will always be a beautiful, voracious child to me, Theria."

Theria slapped his hand away, obviously

infuriated by his comment. A snarling hiss broke free of her lips. "Don't mock me, Abaddon. If I recall, it wasn't that long ago that—" Her words were abruptly interrupted. She snapped her head around; something, someone else, had distracted her.

Abaddon and Siena followed Theria's line of vision toward the massive stone archway as another prepared to enter the torch lit chamber. The dainty redhead darted forward in a blur to prevent the imminent intrusion. Her black cloak sliced through the rancid air, parting the obnoxious smoke with the sheer ferocity of her swift movement. Rage was evident in her penetrating, catlike eyes, eyes that had the ability to paralyze her victims instantly if she desired, rendering them useless. She glared directly into the crystal blue eyes of the unwelcome intruder.

The newcomer was stunning; her unflinching blue eyes held those of the child's. "Well, well, what do we have here, a family meeting? How sweet." She walked around the child and turned her back on the others as she walked graciously along the black marble floor toward the single golden throne.

Their piercing gazes following her, stalking her, as she walked up the seven steps leading to the Royal throne.

Turning to face them once again, Pandora rested gently against the velvet armrest, implying possession. "So, why wasn't I invited to this family soirée? I am heartbroken, how will I ever recover from the pain of rejection?" She chuckled, obviously pleased that Abaddon, who had paused at the bottom of the steps, was unable to read her thoughts. None of their powers, except Theria's, had any effect on her.

"Why, Pandora," Theria hissed through clenched teeth, "I'm sure you will recuperate in bed by wrapping your legs around Cerberus's neck. You may have Cerberus wrapped around your finger, using your body to manipulate my brother at every opportunity you get, but don't you ever dare to have the audacity to think for one second that you are family, that you belong. You are nothing! Cerberus took you in off the street in a moment of weakness, and no doubt by your obvious willingness to please him. Your kind infatuates him, nothing more!" The child's hatred was crystal-clear on her pristine face. If Theria could not have the love and devotion of her elder brother, Lord Cerberus, then no one would, she would see to that one way or another.

Pandora's crystal laughter bounced off the cold stone walls that surrounded them. She stood, raised her hands, palms up, and slowly turned, displaying herself. Her golden ringlets fell effortlessly to her slender waist; her exquisite beauty was undeniable to all who saw her. Clothed in a blood-red gown encrusted with countless diamonds, pearls, and rubies, the strapless bodice of the dress displayed Pandora's perfect breasts. A diamond-studded necklace resembling a spider's web swept effortlessly around her throat and cascaded down her slender shoulders.

Pandora was perfection, the quintessence of beauty. Cerberus did indeed have a reason to worship her. Many envied him his position as Lord of the House; his title enabled him the freedom to bring a human into the Grigori clan.

Theria had objected angrily to her brother, once.

However, she had quickly realized that Cerberus only found humor in her "childish" objections. He had tossed back his head in laughter, humiliating her, calling her a silly little girl. She had swept angrily from the room. He had never denied her anything before. Theria had left Cerberus sitting on his newly acquired throne, one of his leather-clad legs thrown up over the velvety armrest, his laughter ringing in her ears. He had never put a human's needs before hers. She would devise a plan to dispose of the human Pandora. She was not welcome in Theria's world.

"Jealous little one," Pandora whispered now in condescending tones, taunting Theria. "It is no secret that you would like Cerberus all for yourself. The fact that he is your brother means nothing to you, does it? Poor delusional Theria. You will only ever be a child in his eyes, never a real woman—" Pandora froze mid-sentence, unable to move or breathe. Her eyes opened wide with absolute terror as Theria appeared by her side. Pandora remained frozen as the child hovered around her. Theria laughed and glanced at Abaddon as if seeking his permission.

Abaddon, abruptly aware of his little sister's intentions, leaped forward in one bound and grabbed the tiny wrist concealed beneath her cloak. A small silver dagger with an emerald and diamond encrusted handle slipped from Theria's grasp. The sound of the blade echoed around the room as it clattered to the cold marble floor by her feet.

"Release her," he hissed at Theria.

Theria's piercing eyes reluctantly released Pandora. Pandora dropped to her knees and painfully sucked in a heaving breath, filling her burning lungs. She slowly rose to her feet, took a step back, and wrapped herself tightly in her arms. "Half-brother," Theria spat.

Pandora knew the girl had enormous powers. Theria could paralyze her victims on a single whim. She had been foolish to taunt the girl.

Abaddon had known Theria would despise Pandora the moment they had met. Theria was jealous of Pandora, but would she kill her in cold blood? he wondered, intrigued now by the idea. Perhaps he could utilize the hostility between them to his advantage sometime in the future? Smiling, he tucked the idea away.

Pandora, regaining her composure, then glared at Theria. "Don't *you ever* do that again you, vile *little bitch,* or I swear that Cerberus will…"

Abaddon raised his hand to silence her. "Get out of here, Pandora," he roared. "Leave me to sort this out. And please," he implored, "do not bother my brother Cerberus with this tiff. He already has his hands full with this war."

Pandora glared at Abaddon, then shrugged. "As you wish, Abaddon. You have my word. This little annoyance will stay between us. But I warn you both," she began, her eyes flicking from Abaddon to Siena. "Keep that incestuous little beast away from me. Otherwise, she'll have Cerberus to contend with, and not in the manner she'd enjoy."

"Go," Abaddon said once again, his yellow eyes glinting in the torch lit room, "before I change my mind."

Pandora swept quickly down the stairs, along the black marble aisle, past Siena, and out of the chamber, smoke swirling around her gown in a flurry as she departed. Theria was most certainly proving to be a threat to the future Pandora had planned for herself. She would have to come up with an arrangement to rid herself of the girl, and the sooner, the better, as far as she was concerned.

"What were you thinking?" Abaddon boomed at Theria, glaring at her, reading her. "Is it not enough that we fight the Bulguardians, while the city burns below us, that you feel the need to fight, kill, within our family?"

Theria struggled and broke free from his grip. "That woman is not family, not one of us, and I will kill her, drag the lecherous bitch back to the gutter where she belongs. Have you forgotten how this war started?" she hissed at her brother.

Abaddon turned sharply and walked down the black stairs. He had not forgotten.

Siena moved forward and looked up toward the child now sitting tall in the massive throne. "Cousin, there is a time and a place. Now is not that time, nor is it the place."

Theria rose from the throne, materialized beside Siena, and listened.

Siena gently caressed Theria's face in her hands. "When that time does come, and it will, little one, I shall stand by you. You have my word. I will happily cut the whore's throat for you while you watch the blood she is not worthy of drain from her veins, and her face and body decay into nothing more than dusty remains. Although... I do think it more fitting to let her live out her lifetime trapped eternally in the body of a shriveled up old woman. That would be far more painful for her to endure than death. Imagine, little one, when her reflection in the mirror is no longer immortalized in the eternal beauty that Cerberus has bestowed upon her, but instead the face of a sagging old hag."

Theria was euphoric with the images Siena conjured up in her mind. "Thank you, cousin Siena, you are correct, of course, your thoughts are—"

"Ladies, enough of this," Abaddon roared. "We fight a war with an enemy far more threatening than my brother's whore. You must leave now, Siena.

Track down and destroy our enemy. They have all but left the city now. Many have fallen to Earth, scattered far across the lands. Divided, we have the upper hand needed to abolish them once and for all."

"Hunt and destroy the Royal Guard first. Their beloved Pinnacles will be no match for us without their protection. The Royal Guard will blend in very well on Earth; the mortals will be unaware of their existence among them. I sense only a handful of Guards in Altair now, and those I will contend with myself. The City of Altair will then be ours."

"Who will join me in the fall to Earth, Cousin?" Siena asked Abaddon anxiously.

Abaddon watched her as thoughts of the hunt began to quicken her steady pulse. Adrenaline raced through her veins, distracting her elegant poise. Her slender fingernails grew quickly into long, yellow talons. Her attuned hunter instincts awakened within. She restrained herself against the sensations that pulsed through her veins. Closing her eyes for a moment, she relaxed. Her yellow talons slowly recoiled back into perfectly manicured fingernails. He smiled.

"Take as many as you need, Siena," Abaddon answered, pleased at her hunger for revenge. "Your sister, Raven, and your brother, Tyler, take them both. Tyler has become lazy, weak. He needs the hunt to become stronger. You will teach him."

"I will go with you, Siena," Theria announced. "I look forward to entertaining myself with the mortals, I have missed that. They are an enjoyable sport, not to mention an excellent source of sustenance while I hunt and destroy our enemy on foreign lands."

Abaddon was jubilant knowing he would not have to contend with the ongoing self-indulgent battle between Pandora and his sister. His life would be less stressful. He would have further time to indulge himself in pursuits that were far more pleasurable.

"Good girl, Theria. Cerberus will be pleased with your enthusiasm and commitment."

Theria was obviously not pleased with his 'good girl' remark but disregarded it, still swept up in the ecstasy of Siena's plan for Pandora.

"Let it go!" Abaddon implored Theria as he

willed the silver dagger up off the floor and into his outstretched hand.

He sliced the cold blade effortlessly across his palm. A pool of dense, black blood oozing from the wound in his hand before it healed. He extended his bloodied palm to Theria, and she kissed it. Siena did the same. "To family," they chanted in unison.

Abaddon placed the bloodied dagger in Theria's small hand and wrapped her fingers around it. All traces of Abaddon's blood vaporized into the razor-sharp silver blade.

The dagger had been a bequest to Theria from her ailing grandfather. "You will need this on your journey, little one," he had said years ago in their dark underground lair, handing the dagger to her moments before he died.

Abaddon kissed them both; he could taste his blood on their dampened lips. At another time, he would have found the sensation arousing, and acted upon his urges. However, he knew they must go; time was of the essence. He would seek out Cerberus's wife, Pandora. She was always happy to please him, and in so many ways that delighted him.

He kept those thoughts locked away from prying minds. Should Cerberus discover the trysts he had with Pandora in his absence, he could not bring himself to imagine the wrath his brother would unleash upon him. He pushed those thoughts far from his mind. He would plant them in someone else's mind if the need arose. Let someone else be the target of Cerberus's deadly wrath.

Abaddon accompanied Siena and Theria out of the smoky chamber, down a long, wide, black marble hallway to a pair of solid floor-to-ceiling wooden doors. The stone walls, adorned with masterpieces, depicted the beauty that had once been the Imperial City. Abaddon spoke in hushed tones as they floated effortlessly across the cold marble floor.

"Once the House of Bulguardi is defeated, and Empyrean City has been rebuilt to its former glory and ruled by our own, you will both be well rewarded. I will see to that personally. One House, The House of Grigori, will reign supreme. The Bulguardians and their precious Pinnacles will cease

to exist, extinguished. Without their guidance
humanity will turn on each other, and eventually
obliterate themselves from existence."

At the end of the long hall, two guards, dressed
completely in black, stood at either side of the
massive double doorway. Their unmoving faces
portrayed their Mongol heritage. Black inked symbols
adorned their smooth foreheads, a testament of their
eternal pledge to guard Lord Cerberus and the House
of Grigori. The guards turned, bowed their heads, and
pulled open the massive timber doors. A squall of
gray smoke from the burning buildings and souls
below billowed through the doors and swirled around
them.

Abaddon, flanked by the two silent guards, halted
in the massive doorway. Smirking, he watched as
Theria and Siena walked down the torch-lit stone
hallway, their hands clasped together. They continued
onward, their movements effortless, ghost-like, until
coming to a standstill on an illuminated grand
staircase carved entirely in white, polished marble.
Above them, a diamond-encrusted candelabra tossed

rainbow colored shards of light against the raking walls in all directions. The two women glanced at each other, then peered down into the upturned faces in the crowded foyer below.

Abaddon called to them. "One more thing before you take leave..." The two women halted on the staircase and turned to face him. "I want the girl alive!" he demanded.

They nodded and continued down the curving staircase, gray smoke billowing around them.

Abaddon turned and made his way quickly back down the long hallway. The huge doors closed silently behind him. He knew where to find her. She would be waiting for him, as usual.

Pandora was frequently bored, now that her husband, Cerberus, was constantly distracted fighting this gruesome war. She was often eager to find ways to meet her needs, alleviate her boredom. Abaddon met those needs perfectly. Should her husband Cerberus become a fatality, Abaddon would become the next Lord of the House. Her title, 'Lady of the House,' would remain intact. She had no intention of becoming a mere mortal again, standing by hopelessly as she watched her youthful beauty fade with old age. The thought appalled and sickened her. She shivered.

As for Abaddon's needs, he would make do with his brother's wife, for now, until the girl he desired was found and brought to him. The fact that she despised him meant nothing to Abaddon. He did not love her; he did not understand the meaning of real love. His kind was no longer capable of that emotion. He was mad with the desire to possess her, to taste the pure blue blood that pumped graciously through her silky, youthful veins on his hungry lips. Then, none would be able to rival his strength, not even his brother, Lord Cerberus. He, Abaddon, truly would reign supreme. No longer bound by the Principle Laws of the Seven Pinnacles, all would fear him, and bow at his feet. Empyrean, the Imperial City of Altair, would be his to rule.

The dark mass of followers in the foyer began circling the woman and the child.

"Are you ready, little one?" Siena asked.

"Yes, I am ready," the girl replied, an evil smirk spreading wide across her face.

"Then so it shall be."

The masses closed their yellow eyes, bowed their heads, and were gone.

With the roll of the dice, the Fall had begun…. again.

2 – REFLECTIONS

Darwin, Northern Territory, Australia
Year: 2001
The New World

A dainty eight-year-old child sat in the back seat of a restored sky-blue Holden HX Station Wagon as it drove along the hot bitumen road toward the city.

Toward torture, Grace Connors thought, her shoulders rounded in defeat as she concentrated hard on her unsmiling reflection in the shiny glass window of the vehicle. The scenery through the window was nothing more than a vapor of indistinguishable images rushing by in a hurry to go nowhere.

Grace was on her way to ballet lessons. She knew that most little girls her age loved the ballet slippers with the satin ribbons that laced up their legs and the fluffy, pink net tutus. However, she was not one of them; she hated ballet lessons. She sighed, and the face in the glass reflected her emotion. Distaste.

She listened to her parents in the front seat of the car, casually discussing the weekend that lay ahead. Her concentration remained glued to her reflection in the glass window.

Grace was momentarily hypnotized by how ghostly it looked, floating in the window looking back at her. The flashing scenery outside was nothing more than a mass of nondescript blurs.

An apparition, she thought to herself. She liked that word. *Apparition, apparition, apparition*, she said the word to herself over and over. Then suddenly she stopped, aware that something had changed.

The reflection in the glass had transformed somehow. The face looking back at Grace was no longer hers. The face in the glass smiled at her. The reflection wasn't unlike her own, but it was different. The reflection had blonde hair like she had. The girl was about the same age as she was.

Grace put her hand up to her mouth, testing. The reflection did not; it just continued to smile at her. Then the face giggled, imitating the entrancing sound of crystal wind chimes stirred by a flutter of tiny wings.

"Who are you?" Grace asked the giggling reflection in a whisper. She glanced at her parents quickly to see if they had heard her. No response. They continued with their conversation.

'*My name is Hope,*' the reflection answered silently. '*Why are you so sad, Grace?*' Hope asked in a voice which only Grace could hear.

Grace answered in the same manner, only her lips moving to form the words. '*I have to go to ballet lessons, and I don't want to. I don't have any friends there. I don't belong. I hate it...*' She frowned and lowered her gaze, wringing her hands in her lap.

Hope smiled. '*What if I go with you, would that*

make it better, make you happy?' she asked.

Grace's face lit up as if it was Christmas morning. *'Yes. Would you do that?'* she responded silently.

'Of course, but you know that you are the only one that can see me, hear me, you have to remember that. It is our secret.'

"How come?" Grace asked out loud.

"How come what, sweetheart?" her father asked, looking at his daughter's reflection in the rear vision mirror, a big smile on his friendly face.

"Oh nothing, Dad, I'm just thinking out loud," she replied quickly, a tight smile on her face.

Grace hated to lie, but how could she explain her new friend Hope?

The reflection giggled again. *'I'm only here for you, Grace, for as long as you need me.'*

The station wagon pulled up outside the small dance studio. A group of other little girls had gathered outside, waiting for class to begin. They twirled, hopped, and bowed in little pink leotards; satin slippers adorned their tiny feet. Coordination had yet to be learned.

Grace frowned as she watched the other girls, then quickly gathered up her ballet slippers and backpack, and slid out of the car. Perhaps today would be fun for a change, she thought. Perhaps today she would fit in. She shook her head; she didn't want to get her hopes up too high.

"Bye, Mum, Dad, see you later," Grace called over her shoulder as she skipped and giggled her way to the entrance of the dance studio.

"See you in an hour," her mother Kate called back, shaking her head in confusion.

"And I thought you said she didn't like ballet lessons?" Brian said as he watched his daughter with all the other little girls.

A bright light reflected off something his daughter held in her hand. It shone in his eyes, and he frowned as he watched his daughter disappear into the foyer with all the other future prima ballerinas.

Kate smiled and shrugged her shoulders. "Normally she doesn't, maybe she's made a friend?"

"Yes, probably..." He nodded. "Well, that's

good, then. I was wondering when that was going to happen. I'm sure she'll make more friends soon."

Kate looked at her husband with a questioning frown. "I'm sure she will..."

They drove off silently down the street, deep in thought. Kate, pleased that Grace had made a friend at last, and Brian, relieved that Grace would be safe.

3 - HALLELUJAH

"Goodnight, little one, sweet dreams," Brian whispered in Grace's ear that night, as he tucked her up in bed and kissed her goodnight.

"Goodnight, Daddy," Grace cooed, releasing her tight grasp from around his neck. He tickled her, and she giggled.

He made his way to the door, then paused to reach out and touch his daughter's pink ballet tutu, which hung on the back of her door.

"Goodnight," he whispered, knowing only one would hear him. "It's Hope, isn't it?"

'*Yes, it's Hope,*' came the silent reply.

Brian walked from the bedroom, turning off the light as he went, confident in the knowledge that Grace was in very safe hands. *But for how long?* Brian wondered, his confidence wavering. They had all heard whispers. The enemy was hovering, closing in.

When the door closed behind Brian with a click, Grace's bedroom was plunged into darkness.

Hope materialized from the darkness and sat on the end of Grace's bed. Her dainty body emitted a soft glow, dimly illuminating the room. Enthralled, Grace smiled at Hope and sat up a little, resting on her elbows as she listed to every word.

Grace fell asleep that night listening to stories that her new friend Hope told her. The stories were from another time and place, a very long time ago. They would stay hidden within her, locked away safely in her subconscious until it was time for her to remember them.

A gentle breeze danced through the bedroom windows, billowing the sheer pink curtains. Hope slid off the end of the bed, walked over, and covered the sleeping child, tucking a stuffed white rabbit called Bugsy under her slender arm. She walked over and peered through the window and out into the darkness of the night. There was a full moon. Bright stars shone through the rolling gray clouds above.

She stood silently, closed her eyes, shrugged her shoulders, then took a long breath, and exhaled. Slowly, like a flower coming into bloom, small white feathers started to unfurl between her shoulder blades. By the time her magnificent wings had completely bloomed, they had dwarfed her small frame. Hope's eyes remained closed, seeing, hearing.

She could hear Grace's rhythmic breathing as the child slept peacefully in the bed behind her. She heard a news broadcast televised down the hallway in the lounge room.

"A 7.6 magnitude earthquake has hit El Salvador," the reporter announced, "killing at least eight hundred people and leaving thousands homeless. Many still fear for their lives as more quakes are predicted..."

Crickets chirped outside the bedroom window. A frog croaked in a downpipe, signaling rain. Five houses down the quiet, tree-lined street, K. D. Lang sang *Hallelujah* on a radio.

Hope heard a child humming to the same song three blocks away. She could see the small redheaded girl resting peacefully in the crook of a dying old man's arm, just waiting.

His room was dim, lit only by a small bedside lamp and the moonlight that eased its way through dusty floral curtains. An old framed wedding photograph sat on the table beside the lamp. Meager furniture lined the walls. Old family photographs filled dusty picture frames on a set of drawers. The old man slept on a double bed covered with crumpled sheets. An old wheelchair, its paint faded and scratched, sat empty on the left side of his bed, the gray rubber tire tread worn down with use.

The child looked intently at his weathered old face as he stirred and opened his tired eyes, eyes that had seen plenty of this world. Beads of sweat dotted his forehead from the stifling humidity in the tiny room. Reaching out to the man, she brushed away a lone tear from his crinkly gray cheek with her velvety fingers.

Able peered into the stranger's brilliant blue eyes.

"I'm dying, aren't I?" he asked the child in his frail voice, frightened by his words. *Is this beautiful child sitting on my bed Death?* he wondered.

"Yes," she whispered softly. "But don't be afraid, Abel, I will be here with you, I promise," Tia answered, placing her hand on his heaving chest as he fought back his tears and his fears.

He nodded gratefully, consoled by the knowledge that when he exhaled his last breath on this earth, on this night, he would not die alone in this bleak room.

"Would you like me to tell you a story, Abel?" Tia asked gently, sitting up, taking his big, crinkly hand, and squeezing it tightly in her tiny ones.

His hand trembled in hers. These had been strong hands once, he remembered, looking at them. Hands that had lifted his son up high, so he could climb the big flame tree in the backyard. Hands that had taught him how to catch a ball and swing a cricket bat. Hands that let go when he taught his son how to ride his first red two-wheeler bike and catch his first fish. He missed his son, so far away now. He wouldn't get the chance to say goodbye. That was the hardest part. Regret crossed his face when he remembered their last conversation seven years ago. *Seven years ago, seems just like yesterday*, he mused.

"Yes, I would very much like to hear a story," Abel said, closing his eyes. He dragged long painful breaths into cancer-blackened lungs as he listened to Tia's soothing voice.

Wind chimes, he thought to himself.

Tia chanted quietly in his ear, her breath soft against his skin. She squeezed his hand.

"Take my hand, light of day diminish. Fades the sight to hearts held dear. Blue star shine jewel in night. Altair Aquila luminous light. To guide no fear near and far. To sight of Angels, a death held dear. Amun."

Images of Abel's long life flashed through his mind, like a movie on fast-forward on a big widescreen television. He saw his birth, swathed in bright lights, his mother's crimson, sweat-drenched face when placed in his mother's outstretched arms.

When he was seven, sitting on his favorite grandfather's deathbed with a small redheaded girl, the same age that he had been.

More thoughts came quickly. His wife, Rose, giving birth to their beautiful son David—a birth and a death, happiness and pain jumbled together in a time span of moments. His wife's dying breath following the moments that their son David had drawn his first.

He thought now about the girl who sat beside him. He had seen her face before, sitting on his grandfather's deathbed all those years ago? He looked at her flawless ivory face, perfectly framed by long, red hair, then further, into her crystal-clear blue eyes. They appeared to glow like gems in the darkness of his room. Seventy years ago, she had held his grandfather's hand. Now she held his.

Able searched Tia's face for answers and found there an infinite depth of peace. *Yes, it is her, she looks exactly the same*, he realized. He closed his old eyes, knowing it would be for the last time. He had found the answers to the questions he asked when he looked deep into Tia's hypnotic blue eyes. She heard his thoughts. Able sighed out a painful breath. There would not be many more to endured. The constant pain that racked him was now subsiding, leaving his wretched body limb by limb.

Back in Grace's bedroom, Hope lifted her head slightly, the sultry breeze playing with wisps of fair hair that danced across her face. She smelt rain in the air. The sky lit up outside, thunder crashed, and rain fell, bringing with it instant relief from the stifling humidity. Her thoughts went further still. Away for a moment from the bed where Tia held Abel's dying hand, and further. Thousands of miles away, across vast oceans, to the sterility of a New Jersey hospital maternity ward.

Hope heard a woman's guttural cry of pain. It was the type of pain that only women suffer, during the hideously long hours of childbirth. Her husband tried helplessly to comfort her, wiping her hot brow with a cool, water-soaked cloth. Beth had never felt such searing pain.

"Just one more push, Beth," the doctor encouraged in his Scottish accent.

She had pushed with every uterine contraction for the last forty-five minutes. She had endured over twelve hours of labor before that, and now truly felt she had no more to give. Within seconds of these thoughts, Beth could feel her womb torturously squeeze and rise forward within her. Her face contorted, and she screamed in agony as another contraction engulfed her abdomen.

Instinctively she stifled her scream, closed her mouth, and bore down, using what she believed to be her absolute last drop of energy. Immense, burning pain caused Beth to lose her focus, her control. She hissed through clenched teeth, her clawing fingers gripping aimlessly at bed linen, and at her husband's arm, marking him. Her entire body stiffened in sheer agony.

Suddenly the burning, the tearing sensation, and the immense pressure were waning. Her baby was being born right at that moment, and she would soon hold her child. She exhaled and opened tightly closed eyes just in time to see the doctor smile, her tiny baby wiggling and squirming in the doctor's strong hands.

Startled, the woman inhaled sharply. The baby's purple face, covered with a thin filmy membrane, was scrunched up, tiny eyes blinking, little arms and legs flailing.

"Right on cue," the doctor announced, examining the ticking clock on the wall. It was six a.m., the thirteenth of January, 2001. Outside, snow fell, blanketing New Jersey in a thick layer of white.

A cold chill ran down Beth's spine, and her face drained of blood.

"What's wrong with him?" she gasped, terrified that her child had been born dead.

"Ahh, not to worry, Beth," the doctor replied in a jovial, reassuring voice. He wiped the membrane from the child. "Some babes are born caulbearers. Some consider it a lucky omen to be born with a veil, a hood as it's sometimes called, over the wee bairn's face. It tends to run in the family, in the bloodline, so to speak. Nothing to be alarmed about, I can assure you."

The doctor clamped the umbilical cord, and with the confidence born of experience, cut through it with scissors, separating mother and infant. Instantly, droplets of fetal blood stained the glistening blades of the scissors. The fetal blood was the perfect color on the blades before slowly turning the customary crimson color of a newborn infant. He passed the child carefully into the hands of a young African American nurse named Lucina who stood patiently alongside him.

The child gasped and gurgled in her hands as he drew his first long breath deep into unblemished lungs. He cried out fearfully when the frigid air filled his new lungs, burning them.

The child was 'pinking-up' before Lucina's eyes, a reliable indication the boy was healthy. Tiny lungs, squashed just seconds before by the birth canal, were now inflating with oxygen-rich air, and his heart now pumped his blood throughout his perfectly formed body. His gray eyes blinked, trying to adjust his blurred vision to the light-filled room which was now painfully hard to endure after the comforting darkness of his mother's womb.

Lucina smiled down at the squinting child, all arms and legs kicking in the air, before passing him into the outstretched arms of the weeping mother.

After thirteen hours of labor, Beth was exhausted but elated at the tiny miracle she now held tightly at her swollen breast. Both mother and father wept tears of joy for their first-born son.

"He's beautiful," Lucina said as she leaned in and smoothed his cheek with her warm palm. Comfort filled his fearful mind, relaxing his tiny pink face. "What will you call him?" she asked in a soft voice.

"Abe, after David's father, Abel," Beth said, looking up into her husband's beaming face. He was in awe, overwhelmed by this tiny miracle that lay squirming in the arms of his wife. His son.

David kissed Beth's forehead gently, stroking her sweat-drenched hair.

"As soon as Abe here is up to traveling, we are going to Australia so that he can meet his grandfather, Abel. We haven't spoken to my father for a while, so I, my wife and I, thought this would be the perfect time to mend fences, put the past behind us."

Lucina nodded as she watched the happy parents counting tiny fingers and toes on tiny pink feet. She pushed her hands into the pockets of her nurse's uniform and smiled. "Your father is so proud," Lucina said softly.

In Australia, menacing clouds continued to clash. Lightning flashed, fracturing the darkness.

"Godspeed, Abel," Tia whispered into his ear. His trembling lips grew into a peaceful smile. The last image that crossed his closed eyelids was that of the newborn child, his only grandson, Abe and the child's parents, Beth and David—his beloved son.

"Goodbye, my son," Abel whispered. Tia took his big hand; blinding white light engulfed his frail body and lit up his dark room like a beacon. Abel's body vibrated in the stark light as he lay on his bed. Quickly the wrinkles of old age smoothed on his weatherworn skin, the firmness of chiseled muscles of youth returned to his withered limbs. His mind vision flicked, like a fluorescent light coming on behind his eyelids. He was twenty-five again. He was standing on a sun-streaked beach at dawn, holding hands with a young woman. Her long, windswept fair hair blew across her face, concealing her identity from him.

He pushed her hair back so he could see her. His hand paused on her cheek. Her eyes were the prettiest green he had ever seen. But he had seen these eyes before, a very long time ago.

"So, we're grandparents," the woman said, her radiant face smiling up into his handsome one.

"At last," Abel said looking back at his wife, Rose, who was taken from him so many years ago. "I have found you. Hallelujah!" he shouted gleefully, then ever so lightly, kissed her lips. His vision flickered again, and he held his wife tightly in his arms. He would not let her go again. The image in his mind slowly began to fade. He held her tighter. Gone...

The New Jersey hospital room was still now, except for the cooing of proud parents over their son. David stopped counting tiny toes and looked up, confused by what the young nurse had said.

"What do you mean, my father is so proud?" he turned and asked the young nurse, Lucina, but the room was empty.

Just then an older nurse burst noisily through the swing doors, carrying a medical chart and a folded blue baby blanket.

"Hi, Beth, David, and this I believe is baby Abe," she said, marching over to the bed and stroking his little cheek.

"My name is Dorothy," she continued. "Now let's wrap your Abe up, shall we, keep him warm, it's another freezing day outside today."

"The other nurse... where is she?" David asked Dorothy as she quickly wrapped his son.

"Lucina, not sure, could be anywhere on the

ward, lots of babes being born here today," she said, not taking her eyes off the child who now rested quietly at his mother's breast, wrapped firmly in his warm blue blanket.

David kissed Beth's forehead. "I'll be back soon, sweetheart, I'm just going out to let everyone know it's a boy." He left the room as Dorothy chatted quietly with his wife.

"I have a son," he announced proudly to a group of his friends who had gathered in the bustling waiting room. They congratulated him. The women hugged him; the men slapped him on the back and offered him the customary cigar. He declined, remembering how the nicotine had ravaged his father's lungs over the years.

He glanced up and noticed the doctor discussing a medical chart with a young male intern further down the cold hall.

"Gotta go talk to the doc," he said to his friends, excusing himself. "I'll be back." He rushed off down the hall toward them.

"Here he is, the proud new father," the doctor

said, taking David's hand and shaking it firmly. "No big nights out for you for a while," the doctor said, smiling jovially.

"Doctor…"

"David, how many times have we been drunk in the same pub?" the doctor asked his friend. "You can still call me Sammy, even here," he said, waving an arm to indicate the hospital.

David nodded. "Yeah, I know, sorry. It's just that, the nurse in our room, Lucina, she said something and I just wanted to ask her about it." Sammy watched David intently but remained silent. "Lucina, where can I find her?" he asked, looking down the corridor.

"Just saw her leave," Sammy said, turning to point down the corridor toward the glass exit doors.

"When will she be back?" David asked, glancing over Sammy's shoulder toward a window. He noticed that snow continued to fall gently on the rooftops outside. Momentarily he thought about the hot, humid Januarys he had experienced at this time of the year, growing up in Australia. He longed for some of that natural warmth now.

"Won't, today was her last day," Sammy said. "Is there something I can do, another nurse maybe?"

David averted his eyes away from the cold outside. "No, no, nothing like that, it's nothing really, just something she said. I should get back, got tons of calls to make." He took Sammy's hand and shook it firmly. "Thanks, Sammy, I owe you big time, my friend. Gotta go call my dad in Australia, we have decided to name our son after him."

Sammy pulled David toward him and gave him a friendly hug. The smile on Sammy's face faded momentarily. "That's great, now get back to your wife and child, I'll be in to check on you all soon." He pulled away and gave David a friendly slap on the back. "Take good care of that son of yours, Dave. I have a feeling there's something very special about your lad."

David nodded and headed back down the long white corridor, reaching for the phone in his back pocket as he walked. His father would be so happy when he learned that they had named their son after him and that they had made plans for him to grow up in Australia.

He liked the idea of his son growing up with a grandfather. Maybe they could both teach Abe how to swing a cricket bat, kick a football. He dialed his father's number. After all these years, he couldn't wait another moment to speak with his father, hear his voice. "Come on, Dad, pick up."

4 – THE RAINBOW ROOM

Darwin, Northern Territory, Australia

"If happy little bluebirds fly...." Grace sang softly to herself. She walked over to her father who was sitting at the kitchen table; he was reading Saturday's newspaper and drinking coffee from a large mug with the words, 'Golden Eagle Home Delivery Service,' written in bold print on the side.

The breakfast dishes were still on the table; he had promised Kate that he would do them while she was out grocery shopping. He figured they could wait until he had finished reading the sports section of the paper. He picked up a piece of discarded bacon from a plate and popped it in his mouth.

Grace stopped and stood by her father's side for a moment looking up at him, a frown creasing her brow. Then she asked, "Daddy what is a mortaree?" She didn't pronounce the word correctly, but her father knew what she had meant.

A boy in her school, Patrick Wheat, had died, and she had overheard a conversation the older students were having about it during lunch break.

Brian folded the paper and put it down, stalling. He thought about what he wanted to tell her, something an eight and a half-year-old would understand. He pushed back his chair; it screeched in protest against the tiled floor. Picking Grace up, he sat her gently on his lap. He wrapped his arms around her and looked down into her piercing gray eyes. Their mutual devotion for each other was obvious.

"You know, Grace, in some hospitals they call mortuaries," he pronounced the word slowly for her, "the place you go before you go to Heaven to be with the Angels, the Rainbow Room. That is where the little children go that have died, so their parents can sit with them and say their goodbyes. That is where the Angel waits for them. That doesn't sound so bad, does it?"

Grace rested her head on her father's chest and contemplated his explanation and decided that it didn't sound so bad at all. She smiled and gave him a quick hug.

"I love you, Daddy," she said, sliding down off his lap to return to her position in front of the television and eat her biscuits. *I like biscuits; I wonder if they have biscuits in Heaven. They have angel cakes and fairy bread.* She pondered the idea of living on biscuits, angel cakes, and fairy bread. Then she wondered if parents went to a Rainbow Room and waited with the angel when they died so that the children could say goodbye.

Grace considered this notion carefully until Bugs

Bunny jumped up on the television screen and said to her, "What's up doc?"

Giggling, Grace looked over at Hope, who was curled up quietly on a lounge chair. Hope smiled back as she twirled a loose strand of silky blonde hair in her fingers.

Grace wished she could tell her father about her friend Hope, wished he could see her, how pretty she was, how smart. She wanted so much to share this secret with him, even if Hope was just a figment of her imagination. But still, she agonized over not telling him.

Hope, sensing Grace's anguish, hopped down off the lounge chair and made her way over to sit by her friend. She crossed her legs beneath her, smoothed her crisp white Venetian lace dress over her knees, then leaned across and put her arm around Grace's shoulders.

"Grace, your father will understand you not telling him, honestly. He has his secrets too. Everyone does, and that's okay."

Grace nodded and felt a rush of relief, believing

Hope when she said that her father would understand this secret. And Hope was never, ever wrong.

Another thought passed through Grace's mind.

"Are you my Angel, Hope, are you waiting to take me to Heaven?"

"No Grace, I'm not that kind of angel."

"Oh good, because I'm not ready to go to Heaven yet. I'd miss Mum and Dad too much."

"Are you worried about Patrick?" Hope asked.

Grace pictured Patrick with his messy blonde hair and the splatter of freckles sprinkled across his nose and cheeks. He had always been nice to her, and sometimes he would give her one of his biscuits.

Grace held her breath. "Was he scared, when his Angel came to take him to Heaven?" she asked, feeling the weight of the question and fearing Hope's reply.

"Not at all, he was very brave, he was just sad for his parents, he knew how much they would miss him, how they would suffer in their infinite grief. It's an unfathomable thing for a parent to lose a child. Needless to say, it's a loss they never recover from. A parent should never have to bury their child."

Nodding, Grace exhaled and handed Hope a Teddy Bear biscuit. "Teddy Bear biscuits were Patrick's favorite; he always had two in his lunchbox every day at school for recess."

Hope took the biscuit and put it in her pocket. "I'll make sure Patrick gets it okay."

Grace handed Hope another one. "I think he'd prefer two."

"Then two it shall be, and I will make sure he knows they're from you."

5 – ACCIDENT

The word accident is derived from the Latin verb accidere, signifying "fall upon, befall, happen, chance.

Year: 2004

It was a beautiful sunny day in April, April the 22nd, to be precise. The sky was the bluest blue, not a cloud in sight. Mothers pushed baby strollers along the footpath as they walked their older children home from school, listening to their stories. A fresh breeze blew through the trees, sending loose leaves fluttering to the grassy ground below. The wheels on an abandoned pink bike still turned.

Grace was almost twelve, and she had just finished another day at school. She abandoned her bike under the big tree in the front yard and flew through the screen door, letting it bang shut loudly behind her and dropping her school bag on the tiled floor. She moved as if she had tiny wings on her feet, her insides bursting with pure exhilaration. She could barely wait to share the good news with her mother.

Her father, Brian, wouldn't be home today; he was still on week three of a four-week shift at the mine site where he was presently working. He was a consulting mining engineer; he loved the job but missed being away from Kate and Grace for a month at a time. Occasionally his work took him across continents, and then Grace missed him enormously.

She would have to wait and tell her father all about her exciting news during their father-and-daughter phone call tonight. They never missed a night, even when he was far away. She would sit patiently, perched on the tall stool by the wall phone in the kitchen until the phone rang, her thin legs swinging freely beneath her. At six-thirty p.m. on the dot, the phone would ring. She would always answer it on the first ring.

Today, when she ran through the front door, she found her mother in the kitchen as usual.

"Mum, guess what, there's a new girl in my class. Her name is Angela, and she's just moved into the Palmers' house next door, and she has a dog and…"

Grace came to an abrupt halt as though she'd just been hit hard in the stomach, leaving her winded. She bent slightly from the impact of the imaginary clenched fist. The blood drained slowly from her face. An icy chill froze her spine, paralyzing her where she stood. The moment she saw her mother's face, she knew something was wrong—dreadfully wrong. Grace thought she might throw up at any second; she could taste the burning bile making its way up her throat. She swallowed hard to force it back down; it tasted bitter. She pulled a face.

There was a solidly built man in a police uniform speaking quietly to her mother. He seemed to be trying to comfort her. It didn't look like it was working. Not at all. The pain that distorted her mother's otherwise pretty face was resolute.

Kate was seated at the pine kitchen table, staring at the vase of flowers Grace had picked for her the day before. She was crying. Her eyes were red and swollen, as though her tears had burned her. She looked as if she had been crying for a while. She was clenching a tissue in her hand as if her very life depended on it. Perhaps her life did depend on it. There were several more used tissues on the table, scrunched up and discarded.

Before this day, Grace didn't think she could remember her mother ever crying, not like this. These were not the kind of tears one shed over a sad movie. These tears were deeper, heartfelt, palpable. These tears were very real, the result of an unbearable, all-consuming loss. Grace's gut lurched.

"Grace…" her mother said, as she failed in an

attempt to stand. She continued speaking in a whisper, patting the chair beside her, gesturing for Grace to come and sit with her.

Grace dragged one foot after the other; it was harder than it should have been, but understandable since her shoes had just turned to solid lead. Her skinny little legs were barely capable of this usually simple task.

Grace hoped that the longer it took to reach her mother, the longer she could avoid knowing what her mother knew, what her mother was about to tell her. By the look in her mother's pleading eyes, Grace knew that whatever it was, she wasn't going to like it. Not one bit. She sat down cautiously by her mother's side, when all she wanted to do, what her body screamed out to do, was flee. Run as fast as her legs could carry her, to be anywhere but here. Her mind felt numb. Her subconscious mind nagged at her, pushed her. She forced the thoughts back.

Hope reached out for her, but Grace closed her eyes and continued to push her away until she had completely faded out of her vision. She had no time to play with an imaginary friend, not at a time like this. This was serious. This was real.

"Grace, there's been..." Her mother paused, gulped back an urge to cry, still unable to say the words.

Grace shook her head to clear her mind. She tried to focus on her mother's voice, only intermittently taking her eyes off her to glare at the stranger standing by her side, the bearer of bad news that had made her mother cry. Her small hand fumbled absently at her shirt until her trembling fingers found and held the small golden eagle that hung around her neck.

She closed her eyes again, thinking back to a better time.

"To keep you safe, Grace," her father had said on her eleventh birthday, only nine months ago.

"What keeps you safe, Dad?" she had asked, as he placed it around her slender neck.

"You do, Grace, you keep me safe," he had replied, scooping her up and swinging her around and around the room until she had felt giddy and begged between giggles for him to stop. Kate had laughed too, watching them, as she brought in a chocolate birthday cake with pink icing, ablaze with eleven birthday candles.

"Make a wish, Grace," her parents said in unison as they watched her, lovingly wrapped in each other's arms.

She blew out her candles and closed her eyes to make her wish. "I wish that we will always be together, oh, and I need a new bike..." She exhaled; the candles flickered until dancing flames became nothing more than a whisper of swirling smoke.

A giggle echoed through the room, making her smile. Only Grace saw Hope sitting cross-legged on the far end of the kitchen table, clapping. Grace glanced over at her and mouthed a silent '*thank you.*'

An unfamiliar voice crashed through her happy memories.

"Grace," The stranger spoke in a gentle, soothing voice, dragging her back from the happier time. His gentle voice wasted on her. All Grace was conscious of hearing was her heart beating against her chest, trying to escape, and fighting the long imaginary fingers that squeezed forcefully around her throat. She fought for breath. *In, out, in, out*, she told herself. She thought she might pass out at any moment from the lack of oxygen in her lungs.

"Grace,' he repeated, "I am a police officer, but you can call me Wade, okay?"

Grace stared up at him blankly.

Wade took a breath. "Your father -"

Kate held up her hand to stop him from continuing. She closed her eyes for a moment to compose herself. Kate opened her eyes and looked up at Wade, then at Grace.

"Let me," she said. "Grace, your dad…" Kate's throat made a groaning sound. "Your dad was in an accident, and it was a really bad one. There were men trapped in the mine. He went down to help them, but he didn't make it out, Grace. I'm so sorry," Kate whispered as she reached her trembling hand out toward her child.

Grace sat there unable to move, unable to believe, unable to respond, unable to touch the ground with her feet. If she did any of those things, she knew that it would all become horribly real. The words would become a reality, forever. She would be unable ever to go back to a happier time when everything was perfect. A time when her father was still alive.

Her face was emotionless, still, her eyes wide, unblinking. She stared at her mother, hopelessly watching as pieces of her mother began to fade away.

Grace thought that her mother looked smaller, fragile, like a child—like her. They sat hunched together, folded in each other's arms in a dismal effort to support their frail, grieving bodies. She blinked. It was real. She cried.

Kate pulled her closer into her arms with the last of her strength. They stayed that way at the pine kitchen table - with its vase of flowers from the garden and the mounting pile of tissues - until the day turned pitch-black outside. Ghostly black and gray clouds, heavy with rain, quickly engulfed the night sky, blocking out millions of stars from the heavens.

Bolts of forked lightning cracked through the vast darkness of the night. The increasing rumble of unleashed energy rattled the glass louvers violently in their frames. Then the rain started to fall, slowly at first. Then faster, harder. Heavy raindrops, like fists drumming ferociously on the corrugated tin roof overhead. It rained all that night persistently. The stars had closed their brilliant eyes that night and wept, too. Next door, in a brightly lit bedroom of the Palmers' old house, a small dark-haired girl looked across at the dark house, before she turned her face toward the thundering sky.

Wade let himself out the front door, locking it silently behind him as he left. He pulled his coat closed over his broad chest and shoved his hands deep in his pockets. He walked slowly toward his car as the wind and rain lashed at his sullen face.

His senses told him he was being watched. He glanced up and saw the small dark-haired child scrutinizing his every move from the house next door. He lowered his head and continued to walk through the slashing rain toward his vehicle. He opened the door to the black four-wheel drive that he had parked in the street earlier that day and climbed in. He stayed there all that night, guarding the darkened house and its grieving occupants while the unyielding storm consumed the night he sat. He noticed that the girl in the window kept the same steadfast vigil.

At daybreak, a bleak rain was still falling. He scanned the house through the rain-speckled car window; all seemed quiet inside. The girl in the window next door was gone. Satisfied, he turned the key in the ignition and drove slowly away down the wet, deserted street. Rainwater sprayed up over the pavement as he drove through overflowing street gutters.

Grace awoke from a restless night's sleep cuddled close against her mother in the big bed her parents usually shared. She had slept on her father's side. She had fallen tearfully asleep, the scent of her father's cologne lingering in the room reminding her of her painful loss. It was morning she realized, rubbing her eyes with the balls of her fist. Her eyes felt grainy. It was as though someone had sprinkled sand under her eyelids. She heard the rain still beating on the glass window, blurring her vision. She heard the sound of a car driving slowly away down the street. Soon, all that she heard was the rain and the soft rise and fall of her mother's fretful breathing.

Today was the first day of the rest of her life without her father. Her heart had never felt the unyielding weight of such a heavy burden.

She remembered a night only a few months earlier, before her birthday, when her father had still been alive. He had been at home, on one of his breaks. There had been a bad storm that had struck in the middle of the night.

The night had been dark; her room had been even darker.

She could hear her parents' hushed voices in the small Formica kitchen. She turned on her bedside light and pushed herself up on her elbows to listen. Did she hear other voices, too, in the wind as it stole through her bedrooms windows? The curtains lifted in halfhearted objection. Maybe not, she decided.

She heard her mother rush outside and take down the hanging pots that were tangled and overflowed with foliage from the creeping roses. She imagined them swinging back and fro violently in the sudden bursts of wind. She could hear her father bringing in outdoor furniture and anything else that was in danger of being blown around the backyard and into the neighbor's yard. Last time they had had a storm like this, they'd had to fish their outdoor furniture out of the neighbor's swimming pool.

Grace was glad to be tucked up safely in her bed listening to wind shrilling through windows and slamming doors. A flash of lightning made the lights flicker on her bedside table. Moments later the lights went out completely, a power blackout. The storm must have taken down some power lines nearby. She reached for the red and blue Spiderman torch in her top bedside drawer and turned it on, shining it toward her bedroom window. Trees and shrubs were bending and scraping at the glass with their thorny talons, trying to get in out of the wind and torrential rain.

Storms like this were common for the time of the

year. Soon the storm would pass, and in the morning the sun would be burning brightly for the weekend. She turned over and turned off the torch to go back to sleep. She loved falling asleep to nature's orchestra of the wind and the rain as it drummed on the corrugated roof overhead.

Suddenly, a surge of power engulfed her small body, shocking her, forcing her to sit bolt upright, wide awake. She threw off her sheets, ran to her bedroom window and stood there unmoving. She had no idea what she was doing. The static surge of energy ripping through her was so powerful that she could not stop herself. She had no choice but to obey the electric entity that had completely possessed her small body, demanding her attention.

She stood motionless at her window as she watched her father in the dark outside, drenched from the rain. He was retrieving her bike from under the big tree in the front yard, where she had left after school. She should have listened when her mother told her to put it away. A rush of guilt pulsed through her.

She tried to move but couldn't. She was frozen from the inside out, then, with words she had no control over she screamed as loud as she could. "God, somebody help me!"

She felt stupid as soon as the words had left her mouth. She had no idea why she had said that. Bewilderment had her rooted to the spot.

Her father, hearing her distressed scream for help, spun around to face her. He dropped the bike, letting it crash to the ground. He ran toward the house as fast as his legs would carry him. In that same second, a bolt of lightning tore through the massive tree, *boom*, shattering it, spraying the ground with jagged and splintered branches, crushing her bike and missing the intended target - her father.

Kate reached Grace seconds later and pulled her urgently into her arms. Grace shivered against her mother. All she could think about was her bike, her father.

That could have been my father.

Whatever '*It*' was that had taken complete control of her body for those few moments, she realized, *It* had saved her father's life.

The memory of that night was still so vivid in her mind. It still gave her goosebumps to think about it. She rubbed her arms. If only her father could have been saved this time too, he would still be here with her. With her mother. With her family.

Instead, his broken, lifeless body was in a bag, in a cold, stainless steel room, on a cold stainless steel slab. Cold and all alone, while she and her mother shared a big warm bed. A sudden sob broke free from her throat. A tear ran down her face with the thought of her daddy all alone and cold. All completely alone in that horrible cold place.

She wiped the tear from her face. It was her fault, she realized. She had failed her father. She was meant to keep her father safe, wasn't she?

"You do, Grace, you keep me safe." That is what her father had said. And after the night of the storm, she had been foolish enough to believe she really could. She buried her face in her hands and sobbed. Her birthday wish had not come true, only part of it, and she would have traded her new bike for her father in a heartbeat. She had not kept him safe. Would he ever forgive her?

Kate stirred in the bed beside her but did not wake. Grace looked over her mother's shoulder at the framed photograph on the bedside table, of her parents taken on their wedding day. In the picture, her parents were happy. They always were, she mused. They both wore matching white gold wedding bands on their left thumbs. When Grace had asked her mother why they wore their wedding rings on different fingers to other people, Kate had explained that they had just decided that they wanted to be different from everyone else; that their marriage, their union, was special.

She thought about her father's ring. She knew he wouldn't have been wearing it at work. It had something to do with safety in the workplace, so she figured that it would have been safe in his donga with his other personal belongings. She wanted it. It would be her little piece of him to keep forever.

In the morning, a gentle rapping on the front door

woke Grace. She looked over to her sleeping mother, then quietly dragged herself out of bed. Closing the bedroom door behind her, she made her way quietly to the front door, making sure she didn't disturb her mother. She knew that Kate hadn't had much sleep last night, either. She went over to the lounge room windows and peeked through the curtains. Dark clouds were still hanging pregnant in the gray sky outside. The quiet street was empty. The rain was still falling, breeding puddles of despair on the muddy earth outside. She opened the front door a crack and peered out.

Mrs Terran from down the street stood there with a glass dish in her hand, meatloaf, covered tightly with cling wrap. She held her three-year-old son's chubby hand in the other. He had chocolate smeared across his chin. Grace stood still and studied them for a moment, then force-smiled. She opened the door wider and let them in. Hope stood by her side.

"Mum's still sleeping," Grace said in a whisper.

"That's okay, dear, no need to disturb her," Mrs Terran replied in the American accent that, on most days, amused Grace. But not today.

"I'll just put this in the fridge for you," she continued. Baby Abe gripped his mother's dress and toddled to the fridge behind her. Hope followed them and smiled at the boy. The child studied her intently, then grinned back.

"Are you okay by yourself, is there anything I can do for you until your mama gets up? Mrs Terran asked.

"I'm not alone," Grace replied, glancing at Hope sitting up on the kitchen bench beside the fridge. "I mean, Mum will be up soon," she added quickly.

"Well, as long as you are sure. Your Mama has my number if you need me." She looked around the kitchen, scooping Abe up into her arms. He reached out and touched Hope. She held his fingers for just a moment.

"Mama, Angel," Abe said exuberantly.

His mother smiled down into his big round eyes.

"Let's get you home and cleaned up, shall we?" she said, touching his button nose with her finger. "You take care, Grace, and don't forget to call if you need anything…" She let herself out the front door, listening to Abe chatter on about another one of his angel stories.

Grace and Hope stood in the kitchen watching them leave. They waved playfully at the grinning Abe.

6 – THE MUSIC BOX

It continued to rain all that weekend, and all through the week that followed. It rained for nearly a month straight, without any hint of stopping.

Grace thought about death; such thoughts had consumed her since her father's accident. Death haunted her, punished her. Other than a conversation she'd once had with her father, and the occasional dead goldfish, Grace had thought very little about death.

Dead goldfish—that was all she knew about death. Grace liked to believe that a flushed goldfish was happily on its way to a watery fish heaven. The death of a fish was bearable, the loss soon amended by a trip to the corner pet store.

Brian's death, however, was monumentally different. It was painfully unbearable, and unlike a goldfish, he was unequivocally irreplaceable. Her father's death had left her adrift. It had punched a hole in her so great that she could hardly breathe. Later, she would refer to her father's accident as the death of her childhood innocence.

The days that followed Brian's death were made up of a continual blur of acute microscopic seconds, minutes, hours. There were the endless phone calls, flowers, cards, funeral arrangements.

Funeral.

The only other constants were tears and rain.

The days on the kitchen wall calendar rolled over quickly to a miserable Monday morning, the 26th of April. And under cover of a dense gray sky, a child attended a funeral to say her tearful goodbyes to a father whom she had adored her entire life.

She felt like she had been abandoned in a tiny paper boat and left adrift without paddles or an anchor in a bottomless, unforgiving ocean of wretchedness.

A mass of mourners - some she recognized, some she did not - huddled together under an array of umbrellas in the drizzling rain. Grace saw Mr and Mrs Terran holding hands in the front row. The Palmer family, who used to live in the house next door where Angela now lived, were there too, dabbing their eyes with white tissues. They all gave her mournful smiles, even the people she didn't know.

Did they all think of her now as the poor girl with the dead father? The little girl lost at sea in the sinking paper boat? Why not? She did. She did not comply with the formality of returning their sad, desperate smiles. She simply lowered her head from prying eyes and squeezed her mother's hand tighter.

A small redheaded girl caught her attention twenty meters away. The girl walked toward a stone park bench under a big tree and sat down on the wet slab. She was barely visible under the big black umbrella she held above her head. Grace wondered which of the mourners the girl was related. Looked up at Grace, the girl smiled. Not a sad, mournful smile but a smile that radiated peace and joy.

Grace was swept up by an incredible feeling of lightness and peace. She felt as if she were floating. She could see her father smiling at her in the clouds above. She was on the verge of smiling back when the priest spoke, startling her, and stealing her away from the redheaded girl with the infectious smile and the promise of a life filled with joy and happiness.

She felt heavy now—pulled back down into a life wrapped in sadness and death. Back to her tormented life without her father. Back into the tiny paper boat, bobbing up and down on a savage ocean.

She looked back toward the stone bench, but the girl was gone, there was only the priest now, raising his voice over the din of the pelting rain. And the louder the priest spoke, the harder the rain fell. Grace didn't want to listen to his words, words, words.

He continued. "In sure and certain hope of the resurrection to eternal life through our Lord Jesus Christ..."

She didn't want to hear any more.

"We commend to Almighty God our brother Brian, and we commit his body to the ground..."

She wanted to scream. *You did not know my father, he was not your brother, he was my daddy!*

The priest pushed on. "Earth to earth; ashes to ashes, dust to dust..."

Instead, Grace concentrated on the rhythmic drumming of the rain as it pounded heavily on the canopy of umbrellas and the white marquee that sheltered her father's coffin and an array of floral tributes. But the rain merely mimicked the priest's words. Earth, earth. Drip, drip. Ashes, ashes. Drip, drip. Dust, dust. Drip, drip.

"The Lord bless him and keep him, the Lord make His face to shine upon him and be gracious unto him and give him peace. Amen."

"Amen," mimicked the swarm of mourners.

Atop Brian's coffin sat a wreath of red roses and

white lilies, her father's favorites.

"Grace…" She heard her name whispered as the wind swept through the tree branches somewhere in the distance; it was her father's voice.

Blah, blah, blah. More shouted words from the priest as he moved toward her father's coffin. Her mother sobbed gently by her side.

Hope was there now, standing at the head of the mahogany coffin. Raindrops glistened on the tips of her outstretched wings. They fluttered gracefully in a gentle gust of wind. Grace knew it was time to say goodbye to Hope, too. It was a day for goodbyes. A day to say goodbye to imaginary childhood friends. Today was the day she would grow up, putting foolish, childish things away. Her mother needed her now. Hope would understand that, wouldn't she? "I'm sorry, but you have to go now," she whispered to Hope.

"Grace?" her mother asked, "what is it, who are you talking to?"

Grace glanced up at her mother, into her red-rimmed eyes. "No one, Mum, just talking to myself."

She turned back. Hope was gone.

Torrents of rain continued to run off the fabric edges from the ocean of umbrellas and to the muddy earth below. The priest stopped speaking. At last, Grace thought. Just the rain now.

All stood silently by and watched as the flower-adorned casket jolted and then commenced its slow journey down into the sodden, gaping hole in the earth, devouring the coffin that held her father's lifeless body.

Kate wept for her husband and best friend. A little girl wept for her adoring father. Wade stood solemnly by her mother's side, sheltering her, supporting her.

Suddenly Grace panicked and made a quick dash toward the lowering casket.

Her mother gasped and tried to reach out to stop her but Wade took her hand and shook his head. "Let her be."

Grace reached down and with her fingertips snatched up a long-stemmed red rose off the lid of the casket before it slid completely out of reach.

Wade drove them both back home afterward in silence.

It had been a miserable day; it had suited the occasion of death perfectly, Grace decided.

When they eventually arrived home, Grace slid quickly off the back seat of the car and straight into a puddle. Muddy water splashed up onto her leg; she didn't care. She went straight to her room. "I want to be alone for just a while," she had told her mother, the door closing quickly and silently behind her. Her mother had nodded, knowing how Grace felt. She too, needed to be alone.

Grace sat down on her bed next to a box she hadn't seen before and opened it. She lifted out a small, ornate music box with blue birds on the front. Placing the box down on the bed beside her, she unlocked the lid with a tiny silver key. A small ballerina sprang into life and twirled around and around. Tears ran down Grace's face as she listened to the melody the music box played.

'Somewhere over the Rainbow, blue birds fly.'

Grace closed her eyes and said a prayer. "If there

is anyone listening…I just wanted you to know that I'm just a kid. I'm not meant to know about this stuff… death. And I didn't think it was too much to ask to keep it that way, until I'm a grown up, like when I'm fifteen or something. All I want is a mum and a dad. Birthday wishes that come true. It's very hard to believe in blue birds and happiness without my dad. I just wanted you to know that. But most of all, please, please, please look after my dad. Keep him warm. He doesn't like the cold much."

Grace placed the music box on her bedside table and curled up on her bed as she listened to the familiar melody. The mud on her leg left a brown stain on her pink bedspread. By the time the music box had wound down and the melody had stopped, she was sound asleep. She dreamt of her father and the time that he had spun her around and around in her pink ballet tutu. She dreamt of a beautiful angel who held their hands and danced along with them.

Hope pulled the bedspread up over Grace's shoulders and wiped a tear from her cheek. "Goodbye my friend," she whispered. "I shall miss you. But this too shall pass, and soon you'll make new friends and fall in love with a lovely boy, and we shall meet again, in a desert land far, far away.And when we do meet again, you will remember me." Hope's wings bloomed above her head before she slowly faded away. Just a distant memory would remain in Grace's mind of an imaginary childhood friend with wings called Hope. One white feather, the only remaining evidence that she'd existed in Grace's life was all that remained.

A few hours later, waking from dreams about vast sandy lands and majestic dragons, Grace heard voices, lots of voices. She rubbed her eyes, then sat up and listened for a while. *It must be the wake*, she thought to herself. "Stupid word." She wished she hadn't woken, preferring her dreams to her new reality.

She got up, brushed some of the dried mud off her leg and walked slowly down the hallway toward the voices. She leaned against the wall, just out of sight from the unwanted intruders. She smelled the brewing coffee, and the perfume from lavender scented candles. She took a step closer and peered around the corner. Her mother was sitting on the sofa, talking quietly with her friends. She looked awkward. Like she didn't want to be there. Grace knew exactly how Kate felt.

Wade, Grace noticed pleasingly, stood protectively behind her mother.

The group of people mingled around the lounge room eating and talking. Some had overflowed into the kitchen. Mrs Palmer and Mrs Thomson were passing tea and coffee cups around the room on trays. The kitchen table, covered in ivory lace-trimmed cloth, was pushed up against another one to accommodate various plates of food, numerous flower arrangements, and more candles.

A photograph of her father, in an elegant gold frame, was the centerpiece. Recognizing the photograph instantly, Grace's eyes filled with fresh tears, blurring her vision. The photograph was a picture of her father taken on his last birthday.

Mr Terran walked over and sat down beside her mother. His wife, he began, had gone home to take care of their son, Abe. Her mother nodded in response. "Kate," he continued. "Beth and I are so sorry for your loss. Brian was a good man. And we shall all miss him." He picked up Kate's tight ball of a fist. "If there is anything you need, anything, please don't hesitate to call. We are here for you, and Grace, any time you need us."

Kate's other hand crushed a white linen handkerchief with her fingers. "Thank you, David, I appreciate that. Please thank Beth for the food. I meant to call and thank her but..." her voice trailed off and cracked as she blinked back a fresh wave of tears.

"Beth understands that, Kate. She'll come back tomorrow, help you tidy up and help you with anything else you might need."

Kate nodded. "Tell Beth thank you for me." A tight smile flashed across her lips, and then quickly faded.

David stood and pumped Wade's hand. "I'll head off now. I'll be back over the weekend to mow the lawn, weather permitting."

Mrs Palmer walked over to Kate with a mug of steaming coffee in her hand and a small plate of food in the other. Kate thanked her and took the mug of coffee; she declined the food with the shake of her head.

Grace turned away and headed back down the hallway to her room.

She saw the white feather on her bedroom carpet and leaned down to pick it up, stroking it gently with her fingers. She lay back down on her bed, clasping the feather in her hand. "Hope?" she said in a small whisper.

'*Yes, Grace*,' she imagined.

"Nothing," she replied, closing her eyes. And as the day turned into the darkest night, she waited for her nightmares to begin.

7 – TICK, TICK, TICK

The clock kept ticking on the lounge room wall, a constant reminder of the quickening time. Hours became days, and the days turned into weeks, the passing of time reinforcing the knowledge that her father was not coming back—ever.

Grace wanted everything to stop, just for a minute so that she could take a breath. So she would have time to remember her father, before her memories of him spun too far away and out of her reach. But nothing stopped. Everything kept going and going and going.

She had the same nightmare every night. She was living on a spinning carousel. Dead flower petals fell from the sky like rain. Brightly colored horses were racing faster and faster around her. The organ grinder's music became louder and louder. She was losing her balance, grasping at the thin air, trying to hold onto anything fixed in place to balance herself. However, everything she grabbed onto kept slipping out of her hands.

There was a six-foot circus clown with a wide grin and gleaming, barbed yellow teeth riding one of the carousel horses, laughing at her. In the blink of an eye, the clown vanished, then quickly reappeared, floating above her with narrowed yellow eyes glaring down at her. Then suddenly he fell, straight toward her. She spun around; it took forever, that simple task. And then she ran—in slow motion.

She screamed out for her father, who was standing off in the distance, to stop the carousel so she could get off. But he couldn't hear her screams above the music and the laughing clown, so he never came to her rescue.

Every turn of the carousel brought a faceless, shirtless man carrying a bunch of balloons on a golden thread a step closer to her. The balloons were the most beautiful she had ever seen. They glistened like giant soap bubbles, reflecting all the colors of the rainbow.

Finally, when he was close enough to the edge of the carousel, she reached out and grabbed the bunch of balloons from his outstretched hand. The glistening balloons carried her up into the sky, out of the falling petals and into the clouds, away from the laughing clown.

She looked down at the faceless man below as he walked away. On his bare back, she could see a fearsome eagle with outstretched wings.

She was too heavy for the balloons to carry her very far away, and one after the other, they always burst, and she would begin her descent toward an earth covered in a layer of dead petals. She always woke seconds before the deadly impact to find herself twisted in her bed sheets, completely exhausted.

With the passing days, the beautiful flower arrangements delivered following her father's death started to wither and die. Petals faded, shrank, let go and fell onto the kitchen bench, then further still, until they rested on the tiled floor below. One after the other, the flowers gave up their fragile fight for survival, until all that was left were twisted, shriveled stems. Grace gathered up the dead flowers, put them in the trash outside and tipped the foul-smelling water from the vases down the sink.

Blobs of soggy stems and leaves clogged the drain, so Grace jabbed her finger at them, probing them until all remnants had disappeared down the plughole.

She could imagine her father's body progressing in a similar state of decay, under the mound of dirt that separated him from her forever.

She collected up the horde of sympathy cards covered in angels and flowers and put them in a shoebox, with a signed booklet from the mourners who had attended the funeral. Her mother would want these. She tied up the box securely with a white satin ribbon that she had removed from a decaying bunch of flowers.

Kate thanked Grace them put them in the bottom of her wardrobe for safe keeping. She would read them another time when she was feeling stronger.

The hours became days. Tick, tick, tick shouted the clock on the wall as she sat and glared at it. She wanted to stand up on a chair and smash it. Instead, she remained seated and watched her mother dish up her dinner that had been supplied by the neighbors—again. Her mother did not prepare a plate of food for herself. Grace could not remember the last time she had seen her mother eat. She chewed on her bottom lip; she had started to worry about her mother.

Although Kate was now getting out of bed most days, she still didn't appear to be coping with her grief. Even with all the extra food in the house, Grace noticed that her mother continued to grow thinner, and started to fear that her mother might die, too. She began taking mental pictures of her mother for safekeeping. Grace paid attention to little things - like her mother's scent, the sound of her voice. Her laugh, if she was ever to hear that again. Grace welcomed the warmth of her mother's arms as she wrapped them around her, pulling her close. She would memorize everything, just in case her mother was taken from her, too.

She would imagine coming home from school one day, and as she came through the door, standing by the kitchen table would be a policeman. He would say to her, "Grace, there has been an accident." And she would just let herself fall to the floor, wanting to die, too.

Grace slid off the kitchen chair and walked over to her mother, who was washing dishes in the sink. She wrapped her arms around Kate's slender body, squeezing her a little tighter than usual, just in case. "I love you, Mum," she said, forcing back tears. A few still managed to spill over and run down her cheek. She quickly buried her face in her mother's un-ironed t-shirt to wipe them away, hiding them.

Kate dried her hands on her jeans and put her arms around her daughter's shoulders. "I love you too, sweetheart. You and I, we'll be okay, you know that, right?"

Grace squeezed her mother tighter, a frown creasing her forehead. She didn't know that. She didn't know anything, but that didn't mean that she couldn't pretend to, so as not to worry her mother. She'd do anything if it prevented her mother from leaving her too.

There was a rap on the door. Kate kissed the top of Grace's head and went to the front door. Through the screen door, Grace could see Wade standing on the doorstep with a box in his hands and a solemn look on his face. She pushed back the screen door and ushered him in. She offered him a coffee and a seat at the kitchen table opposite Grace. He pulled out a chair and sat down, declining the coffee with a shake of his head.

Hesitantly, he placed a brown box on the table. Scrawled on top of it in bold handwriting was 'Brian Connors — deceased.'

Kate sat down rigidly at the end of the table and eyed the box. Wade slowly pushed the box across the table toward her. For a moment Kate just looked at it, reading the words. A tightness gripped her throat, her stomach lurched. She took a deep breath and held it. Slowly, she removed the lid to reveal the precious contents neatly packed inside. She reached in slowly and ran her fingers over the items. She let out her breath, let out her tears, silent tears that ran shamelessly down her face.

She took out folded t-shirts and jeans and placed them on the table beside the box. She found Brian's gold wristwatch and turned it over in her trembling hand. She silently read the elegantly engraved words, 'My eternal love always, Kate.' She placed the watch carefully on top of the clothes folded on the table. Underneath another t-shirt were a mobile phone, toothbrush, hairbrush, Bvlgari aftershave, and a black notebook. Her eyes darted around the emptying box. Her frenzied fingers probed eagerly between the folds of fabric, the corners of the box. She began to search more urgently, searching pockets, seams. Nothing.

Kate's search was proving fruitless. Her husband's wedding ring was nowhere to be found. A sudden sob escaped her lips, and she covered her mouth with her hand to stifle those that would follow.

Wade raked his fingers through his hair, feeling guilty for making her cry again. He so badly wanted to reach over and console her, but he refrained, fearful of what might happen if he did.

Grace walked over to her mother and put her arms around her to protect her against the fresh, consuming grief.

Kate nodded. "It's okay, really… I just need to… I'm sorry…" she said, standing. She quickly placed Brian's belongings back in the box and replaced the lid. She stood there unmoving for a moment, staring blankly at the box. Wade stood and took a step toward her. "Kate-"

"Don't," she snapped, then felt instantly guilty for the bitterness in her tone. "I'm sorry, I can't…" she dragged the back of her hand across her wet cheeks, picked up the box, and walked out of the kitchen, down the hallway to her bedroom.

They stood there and watched her go, watched her disappear into the darkness of the room as she closed the door quietly behind her.

Kate sat down on her bed and placed the box beside her. After a moment, she removed the lid and pulled a folded shirt from the box and buried her face in the folds of fabric. She pulled in a long breath, filling her lungs with Brian's familiar scent. She could hear him teasing her for being silly. Like when she would cuddle up next to him on the sofa, burying her head in his chest because she had been crying at a sad movie. "I can't do this without you," she said, sobbing uncontrollably into the shirt. Wade wrestled with the urge to follow Kate, put his arms around her, hold her close to his heart, and tell her he would be there for her. Instead, he walked over to the kitchen bench, picked up the plate of food that Kate had prepared for Grace and put it on the table. "Here, Grace," he said gently. "Sit down and have something to eat." Grace sat down submissively, picked up a fork and watched as her tears dripped onto her plate.

Grace never thought to question Wade's being there. And why would she? She needed someone –

anyone - who would care for her while her mother could not.

Wade busied himself with making coffee, then sat down opposite her and watched as Grace pushed the food around on her plate. The fork looked enormous and cumbersome in her tiny hand. Her little face, with its big, watery gray eyes broke his heart. He knew he deserved to suffer the pain that tore through him. He alone had broken the hearts of this mother and her child.

That was when Wade, against his better judgment, decided to stay, for just a while. He would try, as best he could, to put some of the broken pieces back together again. He owed them that much. The truth, though, could only do more harm than good, so that, he would keep to himself.

He wasn't sure how long they sat there like that, listening to the heartbreaking sounds of Kate's sobbing drifting softly down the hall.

8 - KALI AND BONGA

On a cold, wretched Sunday morning in June, Grace woke to yet another wet, colorless day. It had been raining consistently for weeks, without any hint that a change was drawing any nearer. Grace felt agitated by the smothering, gray sadness that had shadowed her constantly since her father's death.

She decided that she had had enough of her miserable existence behind the cold steel bars of grief. It was up to her alone to make the necessary changes to rectify the problem.

She pushed the blankets away and swung her legs enthusiastically over the edge of her bed. Her pathetic life, coupled with the gloomy weather, had become too depressing and predictable.

But something was already a little different about this morning, Grace sensed, with a hint of trepidation. She frowned when her stomach growled. She felt something she hadn't felt for a while. Really, really, hungry, with an unyielding urge to hunt down food and eat.

Grace felt sick with hunger as she stood; her legs trembled uncontrollably. She crouched down onto her haunches to steady herself and clutched her stomach. She looked up toward the ceiling, which started to vibrate and blur. Snowy white dots, like a dysfunctional television screen, filled her vision.

"Oh no, not again," she whispered in a frightened voice, just before her legs gave way and she collapsed on her bedroom floor.

As Grace's eyelids flutter and close, her mind drifts

into a fitful dream, my own eyes open, and I realize that I am not the Juliette I last remember, but a younger girl, from an earlier time and place.

My mouth and tongue are parched, devoid of saliva, and it hurts when I try to swallow. My lips are dehydrated and cracked, resembling an old, worn-out, brown leather belt. A kitten meows on the ground beside my filthy bare feet.

"Bonga?" I say in a small raspy voice as I reach down to stroke the skeletal animal. I study my bony fingers, which are now almost alien to me. I try to rub mud off my hand with equally dirty fingers. I gasp when I realize that it isn't dirt that coats my body.

I search my memory for answers and realize that I have returned to Bengal, and it is 1769. I am re-experiencing the wretched suffering of myself as an eleven-year-old brown-skinned girl. An obnoxious stink assaults my nostrils, making me gag. I don't smell good. Nothing, in fact, smells good. The soiled walls surrounding me emit a foul-smelling stench of excrement, urine, and rotting flesh. I cover my nose and mouth with my grubby hand, but it doesn't help.

"Kali, stay here with your mother, I will return with food by nightfall," a man says to me in a foreign language that somehow, I understand.

I nod obediently. Maybe tonight father will bring home a rat, and we will eat like kings. Father is tall, softly spoken, and frightfully thin. He is dressed in dirty clothes that resemble rags. Starvation has robbed him of his looks and his strength, leaving him haggard and defeated. Only the love and devotion he feels for our family keeps him alive, day after day. I know this truth about him, and it makes me love him even more. My heart is bursting at the seams with love, my stomach bloated but empty.

I remember a time, not that long ago when he was handsome, strong, well-dressed and wealthy for a man of his station in life. A prosperous and respected merchant trader, trading in textiles, tea and exotic spices throughout India and foreign lands. We had wanted for nothing.

I watch him now as he prepares to leave; intuitively, I know that I will never see this man again, and it saddens me. A dirty tear runs slowly down and over my protruding cheekbone.

"Goodbye, Father," I say as he trudges away. "I love you." He doesn't hear me; the bustling noise outside our tiny hut has already swallowed him up.

My kitten Bonga shrieks loudly in protest behind me. I spin around in time to see a girl snatch the kitten up from the floor by its oversized head. The girl snarls and threatens me with her wild yellow eyes, her teeth bared. In one swift movement, she twists the kitten's scrawny neck, breaking it. It dangles silently in her hands as the girl turns and flees quickly out into the dirty alleyway. My kitten, Bonga, will be an appetizing meal for four this evening.

A woman's voice behind me says, "Kali, come."

This woman who summons me, I know instinctively, is my mother. My heart swells with unbounded love for her. She is lying on dirty rags on the floor and looks like a beautiful skeleton draped in satiny brown skin. By nightfall, I know my mother will be dead, and I will be alone in this place.

So will ten million other men, women, and children. They will starve to death during one of the worst famines in history during the 17th century. It will happen again.

I lie down beside my mother and close my eyes. I pray for a quick walk through the valley of the shadow of death. The Gods smile down upon my mother and me this night. We do not have to wait long before the child-like Angel, with her crystal-clear blue eyes and long flowing red hair that shines as though it is on fire, holds our hands and walks us home to a beautiful place far from here.

Awakening on the carpeted floor in her familiar bedroom, Grace slowly blinked and opened her eyes. Brushing tears from her face, Grace's thoughts lingered on the brown-skinned girl called Kali and her parents. They were all dead now; their brown bodies had decayed into the parched cracked earth over three hundred years ago. She thought about Bonga, too, the Bengali kitten, dangling from the hands of the yellow-eyed girl, his neck limp and broken.

Grace rubbed her eyes to erase the brutal images and memories. The dreams and visions she had experienced from an early age were occurring more frequently now, and where they had once dissolved as quickly as they had manifested, they now lingered a little longer.

I need to eat, Grace thought, standing slowly, her legs still trembling.

She inspected herself carefully in the mirror from head to toe. She pushed the long flannel sleeve up to her elbow, examining the color of her skin. She was clean, she was white skinned, she was back — she was Grace.

9 – ANGELA OAKS

Before food, Grace decided she had to deal with the incessant rain that had become her jailor. The constant rain had trapped her in a watery prison of self-pity.

She realized that this was not how her father would have wanted her to exist. Not at all. She had served her time with the demons in Purgatory. She had to do something, had to chase the demons away, be free. There was a path out there somewhere that she was supposed to be on, she knew that. She also knew without any doubt that this was not it.

"You can do this, Grace, I know you can," her father would have told her. "Come on, get up, try again."

"Okay," she said to the voice in her head with vigor. "I can do this!"

She ran barefoot outside into the pelting rain in her pink polka-dot flannelette pajamas. She would make a change. Her father would indeed be proud of her. She sprinted through the front door and out into the yard. Then she went down, hard, tripping and falling on her hands and knees, mud splattering over her face.

She looked up into a gray sky that loitered persistently overhead.

"Enough, stop raining!" she demanded. Then passively, "please."

A contemptuous flash of lightening, followed by the heavy rumblings of thunder, pulsed through the angry sky in response to her plea.

The rain continued falling, flowing over her as it

plastered her long hair to her muddy face and dripped off her dirty chin. She dragged herself to her feet, hung her head and plodded through murky puddles back into the house, defeated.

She closed the front door behind her with an angry shove, and trudged down the hallway, leaving muddy footprints in her wake. Her grand plan to create change in her life, an undeniable failure.

By the time Grace reached her bedroom, pinpricks of sunlight had flickered, then punched their way through the ominous gray clouds, scattering them in all directions like bowling pins. Then, slowly, the rain began to subside, until only occasional heavy droplets of rain fell haphazardly to the ground from the branches.

Grace glanced out of her bedroom window and marveled at the brightest rainbow she had ever seen. The luminous colors were dazzling as they arched high across the blue skyline.

"Skies from heaven, Dad," she said out loud as she pressed her hand against the window.

That is how her father would have described the

phenomenon to her when he saw the sky looking like this.

Grace's lips rolled up slowly into an ever-so-slight smile. *Maybe dad sent the rainbow, to let me know he's in heaven*, she thought wistfully to herself.

A sudden movement closer to earth caught her attention. She noticed Angela, her new neighbor, walking expertly along the top of the high timber fence that separated the two yards. The girl glided effortlessly along the fence, like a model on a catwalk. Then she paused, pivoted, and jumped down to land elegantly on the ground, like a gymnast exiting parallel bars. She landed perfectly on the ground beside a small white dog and began walking toward Grace's back door. The dog followed obediently at her feet.

Grace rummaged through her drawers until she found a pair of faded denim shorts with rhinestone studs along the pockets and a bright yellow t-shirt. She dressed quickly, then scraped her wet hair off her face and secured it with a large sunflower clip. She snatched up her saturated pajamas from the end of the bed, used them to wipe the mud from her face and hands, and then tossed them onto the floor.

Her stomach growled again, reminding her that she desperately wanted something to eat. She darted to the back door and pushed it open. Angela and the white ball of fluff stood rigidly on the doorstep.

Grace grabbed Angela's arm and pulled her urgently inside.

"Are you hungry? Good, let's eat," she said to the bewildered Angela in a hurried voice, not waiting for an answer. She kept a tight grip on Angela's pale arm and dragged her along the hallway into the kitchen. She deposited Angela in a seat at the kitchen table as if she were a rag doll. Hurrying over to the fridge door, she hauled it open and marveled at the delectable bounty filling the shelves. "Bonanza!" she shrilled, throwing her arms up into the air with jubilation.

Grace couldn't remember a time that she's seen so much food in their refrigerator. The shelves were full, crammed with food from the neighbors. She gathered up an assortment of food and shoved loaded plates on the table in front of Angela.

"Dig in," she said. "Are you starving too? Here, have something to eat," she said pushing bowls of food toward Angela. The dog yapped, so Grace gave him some chicken; there was plenty to go around.

"No, I am not starving," Angela replied promptly with wide eyes. "I eat food regularly that contains nutrients, vitamins, and minerals to prevent starvation and malnutrition." She eyed the streaky mud on Grace's face. "You have…" she said, pointing her finger at Grace's face. "Mud."

Grace looked over at Angela; almost hidden from view by a large slice of watermelon sitting on the platter in front of her. "Yeah, it's nothing, have something to eat."

Angela picked up an apple from the fruit bowl and nibbled at it. Like Bambi, Grace thought, her face breaking into a smile. She turned to looked at the dog. "What kind of dog is that?" she asked as she watched the small dog sitting at Angela's feet with his pink tongue dangling out.

"Champ is a West Highland Terrier, a native of

Scotland and commonly known as a Westie," Angela answered, and then continued. "The breed was used to seek and dig out foxes, badgers, rats and -"

"Okay," Grace said interrupting her, "I got it; Champ is a West Highland Terrier, Westie for short." She paused for a brief moment, "I'm so hungry I reckon I could eat a rat..."

Angela raised her eyebrows. "That is hungry, but you shouldn't. Rats carry numerous parasites and germs."

Angela had big, round, innocent, fawn-like eyes, with long, dark lashes. But instead of her eyes being the usual brown of many dark haired people, Angela's eyes were the most amazing shade of violet. Her thick, silky hair fell like a veil of black satin across her slender shoulders. Her oval face was ivory smooth, with a blush of color on her cheeks. Rosy cherub lips formed her spoken words perfectly, too perfectly. Words that you could imagine hearing from someone much older. Not from an eleven-year-old child.

"It's just an expression," Grace said. "I'm not

actually going to eat a rat." But she couldn't say the words with conviction. Had she eaten a rat before, she wondered? She shuddered with the ghastly thoughts that suddenly flashed through her mind.

Grace stood a good head taller than Angela. One could easily be mistaken for thinking that Angela's elf-like build indicated a vulnerable child. However, one would be very sadly mistaken about that.

They sat eating quietly for a few moments until Grace said, "do you want to watch a movie? I'll put one on if you like. I've got lots of DVDs."

Angela stopped chewing and frowned, not sure how she should respond to this question. Or was it a statement? Humans, so many rhetorical questions. "Is that a rhetorical question?" she asked, just to clarify.

"Rhetorical question? I'm eleven. I don't even know what that means," Grace said, then continued with a mouthful of food, making it hard for Angela to understand her. "Do you own a bike? I know a really cool place if you'd prefer to go for a ride?" She paused for a moment to swipe a piece of chicken off her chin. "My bike is new, the last one I had got smashed during the thunderstorm. The tree in the backyard fell on it - *BOOM*!" She clapped her hands together for effect, then gently persuaded an errant piece of meatloaf into her mouth with her thumb.

Angela, momentarily startled by Grace's sudden clap of hands, looked up from behind her apple. "A movie sounds splendid; I'm not in possession of a bike, nor do I like bikes," she said, placing the barely eaten apple back on the table.

Grace nodded and swallowed another piece of meatloaf. "Okay then, a movie it will be. I'll go find one and get it started while you bring the food over."

Grace hopped off her chair and went into the lounge room to search for a movie. She left the motionless Angela staring hesitantly at all the uneaten food still piled in front of her on the table.

Does she intend on eating all of this food? Angela wondered, contemplating her present predicament. She realized that she was totally unaware of just how much food this child would need to appease her evident feeling of starvation. Her body didn't appear to be undernourished.

Grace came back to help with the food. "Come on, Angela, get a wiggle on," she said, grabbing various plates of food from the table. Angela slid off her chair and followed Grace, without the wiggle.

They placed the plates of food on the carpet in front of the television and sat cross-legged watching movies for the next three hours. They watched, listened, and learned. Angela did most of that. They ate, talked, and giggled. Grace did most of that.

Grace learned that Angela's parents were both shift workers, so Angela was left to fend for herself most of the time. This fact didn't seem to upset Angela as she spoke of it; in fact, she appeared to prefer her solitary existence. Angela spoke with an unexpected knowledge and confidence, and then at other times, she became distant and withdrawn, as if she were no longer in the room.

Angela, Grace decided, was a little odd, almost like an old person in a young body.

"An assortment of fascinating contradictions." That was how her father Brian would have described Angela.

Angela either frowned or smiled as she studied Grace with total fascination, learning everything about her. She <u>learned</u> about the things that made Grace happy, and what made her sad. How her forehead would furrow as she wiped away a tear with the back of her hand when she spoke of her father. How much she missed him. Angela quickly <u>discovered</u> how much food Grace could consume before she declared she was stuffed. She took this to mean that Grace had eaten an adequate amount of food to ward off her feelings of starvation, for now.

Grace talked about her mother, who still cried herself to sleep each night. The ballet lessons, which she had quit going to since her father had died. She didn't feel like dancing anymore.

Grace thought briefly about Hope, random images of her friend fleeting through her mind. Her attention shifted, the images fled like a feather swept quickly away in an impetuous flurry of the wind along a deserted sidewalk.

Grace focused her attention back to the present - to Angela - and talked about school. They would walk to school Grace had decided when learning that Angela didn't own a bike.

"You're in my class at school you know, I saw you when you came into the room, and Miss Bell introduced you to the class."

"Hmm."

"Maybe you could sit next to me on Monday. If you want to."

"Yes."

"Well, it's just that I don't have any friends, and you're new so… maybe we could be friends, what do you think?"

"I concur," Angela responded, and then tried a smile; it seemed like the appropriate response.

"Concur?" Grace said, squishing her face into a frown.

"Oh, yes, I mean yes, I agree, friends would be good, we will sit together."

Angela made a mental note to try and think like an 11-year-old child. It wasn't going to be easy. Nothing about being human was easy. Mortals, she decided, were such a complex race of beings, with so many illogical inconsistencies and idiosyncrasies.

"Great, I'm so glad," Grace said, beaming. Having a friend, she decided, would make the long school hours bearable.

"Would you like me to paint your fingernails?"

Angela studied her nails; they appeared to be the correct color. "Yes?" she replied. More in the way of a question than an answer.

"Great, what color? I've got lots," Grace said running off to her room to find her box of fingernail varnish.

Grace sat and busied herself with coloring Angela's nails while they watched their movie. "There, what do you think?"

"Well," Angela said hesitating, and trying not to look too mortified at the color covering her nails - and cuticles. "This is very colorful, isn't it?" She looked at each one of her painted fingers in turn. Each one was a different color from the first. In the center of each brightly colored nail, Grace had stuck a small round smiley face. "Not at all what I expected, but thank you… I think."

"Mum says I'm very creative," Grace said, studying her workmanship.

"Creative… yes, that is one way of looking at it, I suppose." Angela sniffed the strong-smelling liquid on her fingers and screwed up her nose. "It doesn't smell very nice, does it?"

"Okay, your turn to do mine," Grace said, thrusting out her hands out toward Angela.

"Oh, I'm pretty sure I don't do creative," Angela said with a horrified look on her face.

"Oh come on, I did yours. Now it's your turn to do mine. Or," Grace said unfolding her legs out from under her, "you could paint my toenails." She wriggled them enthusiastically at Angela.

"Fingers," Angela announced, unscrewing a bottle of pink glitter varnish.

And so, it was on this sunny Sunday, watching television with Angela and painting nails, that Grace's heart began to heal. It was also from this day forward that Grace and her odd little friend Angela became inseparable best friends.

"I'm pretty creative with hair, too," Grace said,

admiring Angela's satiny shoulder-length hair. "Do you want me to-"

"Definitely not," Angela said shaking her head frantically.

"Oh, come on... let me just try this one thing," Grace said, picking up a pair of scissors.

"Woops," Grace muttered as they watched a clump of Angela's fringe fall to the floor in front of them.

10 – A SECRET BOUND BY BLOOD

The roles between Kate and Grace changed dramatically during the days that inevitably ran headfirst into the weeks, then months, following Brian's death. Grace comforted her mother, as though Kate had been the frail child suffering from the loss of a beloved father.

Then, when Wade disappeared, leaving her alone to cope with Kate, and her own crippling grief,

Grace's demons began to circle once again.

Grace missed Wade's comforting presence during her torturous, nightmare-filled nights. She missed him watching over her, like an angel rising from the depths of her darkest shadows to protect her and guard her against hungry demons. He had been there for her when her dreams had made her scream out into the still of the night. He had held her heaving, broken body tightly against his chest until her tears, and the raging storms outside subsided.

In the morning, while Kate slept in her self-induced coma, Wade would prepare breakfast for her before she left for school. She would always wave goodbye to him happily, knowing he would be there waiting for her when she returned.

Grace would run through the front door after school to find Wade. But on this day, as she ran into the house, he was not at his usual spot at the kitchen table, drinking coffee.

She called out to him, "Wade..." but there was no answer to push the creases from her brow. But denial can clasp your hand at the darndest of times, and lead you slyly down the well-worn path to impossible hope.

"Oh, I get it; we're playing hide and seek…" she called out as she twirled herself around. Mocking faces from photographs smiled out at her from picture frames hanging on the walls.

"You can't hide from me forever, you know, I'll find you…" She ran behind the sofa, nothing. She ran through the house, searching each of the rooms in turn. All but one. She avoided her mother's room. Kate would probably still be curled up in bed under the sheets; either hiding or asleep. Grace was never sure.

Behind the laundry door, searching. Still nothing. Grace ran down the hall to her bedroom and leaped inside with her arms outstretched. "Ta-da! I found you!" she squealed, but the room remained unmoved—silent.

No Wade. No Hope. Who would tell her now that if everything was going to be okay?

That was when she saw the leather-bound book on her bed, with 'Grace' etched in gold on the front cover. She traced her fingers over the gold letters, then opened it and read the handwritten inscription inside.

Grace, A secret bond bound by blood.

Forever.

Wade.

She read it again, this time out loud. Perhaps the answers she was looking for would come to her if she read the words out loud.

She opened her palm and looked at the fine lines in her hand, lifelines. There was no visible mark where a small scar should have been. Was that an answer? Or was it just another unanswered question to a riddle?

She sat on her bed and hugged the journal to her chest. She knew then that Wade had left her; she only hoped that it wouldn't be for too long. She needed him. She wiped a tear from her cheek. Inside, her soul screamed the scream of a thousand circling demons.

As time passed, less and less did Grace have to coax her mother out of bed every day. Occasionally, though, she still had to remind her mother to eat, bathe, brush her hair, her teeth.

Angela became the shining beacon that lit Grace's way along the dark path left by Wade's unexpected departure. She would come over before school every day to have breakfast with Grace and sometimes, the lifeless Kate.

After breakfast, Angela would clean up the morning dishes while Grace strode off to her bedroom to dress for another school day.

On these mornings, after Grace had finished dressing, she would watch Angela sitting beside Kate on the old sofa in the lounge room, Angela's tiny frame almost engulfed and swallowed up between the soft, plump cushions. Angela's little dog Champ, as always, sat loyally at her feet. His tiny, round, black eyes, almost unblinking, watched Angela attentively.

Angela would converse with Kate in soothing musical tones. However, it wasn't the words Angela spoke, more the way that she voiced them through rosebud lips, which was hypnotically soothing to the listener's ear. Harps, Grace thought, when she heard

Angela murmuring softly to Kate.

Grace never knew what Angela and her mother spoke of, but whatever it was, it was helping. The friendship that grew during this time between Kate and Angela felt somewhat unusual to Grace, misplaced. But the feelings began to pass quickly as her mother began to awaken from the depths of darkness.

Grace let out a sigh. "I'm ready for school when you are, Angela," she said, wriggling into the shoulder straps on her backpack. She walked over to her mother, bent down, and kissed her gently on the cheek. "See you after school, Mum."

Kate gave her a weak smile in return as she brushed her fingers lovingly down Grace's cheek.

"I'll be here, waiting. I'll make something special for dinner..." She forced a reassuring smile; it didn't reach her sad, hollow eyes.

"That sounds great, Mum. See you when I get home," Grace said. "I love you."

"I love you, too, sweetheart," Kate said from the safety of the old reliable sofa. "You two girls have a good day, okay? I'll see you here after school."

Champ yapped, jumped up on the sofa beside Kate and dumped his head in her lap.

The girls waved to Kate as they walked through the door, Grace leading the way. She appreciated her mother's genuine attempt at sounding somewhat capable. But she knew that it would most likely be baked beans on toast again that night for dinner. Baked beans on toast or pizza, both had become staple evening meals at the Connors household, after the prepared meals from neighbors had run out.

"Your mother is getting stronger every day, Grace, it won't be long now before she is back to being her usual self," Angela said gently, running her hand down Grace's arm. She could feel the fiery crackle of energy burning her fingertips, which steadily increased as Grace's evident despair grew.

Grace sighed, "I thought she was getting better, then…" Her voice was swept away by a brisk flurry of the wind that twisted loose leaves around her legs as she walked. A streak of glass lightning, then thunder clapped and fractured the cloudless sky overhead.

Angela pushed Grace along the sidewalk, through the squall of leaves.

"I think sometimes your mum just has days that are worse than others. That's all. What do people call them, these bad days?"

Grace looked at Angela with a serious frown, and then slowly the expression on her face changed, and she broke down into fits of laughter. She gripped her stomach to try and contain herself. She had to admit, though, that it felt wonderful to laugh out loud like that again.

"They call them bad hair days," Grace said, trying to control herself as she looked down at Angela. A huge clump of hair was still absent from her otherwise perfect fringe.

Angela glared back at her with a stern look that looked misplaced on her angelic face.

Grace held her hand over her mouth in an attempt to conceal the remaining grin.

"I'm so sorry, Angela. It's just that, well, it's a bit funny, you have to admit," Grace pleaded.

"So everyone keeps telling me," Angela mumbled under her breath as she strode forward, kicking the drifts of leaves lying on the path and swinging her arms fiercely by her sides, leaving the stunned Grace in her wake.

"Oh, come on, Angela, it was an accident. You weren't meant to move your head," Grace said, jogging to catch up. She threw an arm around Angela's shoulders. "It'll grow back—eventually. One day we will laugh about this."

Angela's face, although still plastered with a stern frown, hid a secret smile. Grace's skin no longer burned with the unrestrained energy that had, only moments ago, radiated dangerously from her body.

The wind had completely settled, leaving in its wake a trail of random leaves scattered across the ground. The sun shone encouragingly in the clear blue sky above as they walked down the footpath toward school. Sunshine sliced through the dense blanket of despair that had draped itself uninvited over Grace's world.

Grace watched as a boy walking a few meters

ahead of them rounded the corner, and gave Angela a little nudge with her elbow.

"What was that for?" Angela asked rubbing her arm, checking for a bruise she knew she wouldn't find on her ivory skin.

"That's Joshua Deneb."

"Yes, that's Joshua Deneb. I know that. What is the point you are trying to make, Grace?"

"He likes you," Grace said matter-of-factly, a grin on her face. "Should we run and catch up with him?"

"No, Grace. I am perfectly happy to walk at this pace, which, by the way, should get us to the school gate approximately seventeen minutes before school commences."

Grace laughed and shook her head. Angela was always so funny. Seriously funny, she thought—in a non-intentional way.

Angela continued with her spiel. "As long as we are all heading to the same destination, we will all, eventually catch up.

"Okay, Angela, we can do it your way," Grace

replied happily.

Angela was, of course, correct. She usually was. They arrived at the school gate sixteen minutes and fifty-nine seconds before the school bell sounded.

Josh was kneeling at the gate when they arrived, waiting and pretending to tie his shoelace. He blushed, his cheeks turning red when they came to a halt in front of him.

Angela, with her arms folded across her chest, glared at him and said, "why are you untying then retying your shoelace, Joshua Deneb?"

He rose, shoved his hands in his pockets, shrugged, and then failed to prevent the infectious grin that whipped itself across his good-looking face. Joshua gazed at Angela, transfixed by her dazzling violet eyes. She was the most beautiful girl he had ever seen. He blushed as she returned his gaze, a frown creasing her brow. "Come on," Grace announced, tugging on Angela's arm. "Let's get to class."

The three friends turned in unison and headed toward their classroom, Joshua's persistent gaze fixed firmly on Angela.

The days continued to slip by, and Grace began to see glimpses of a future where she could be happy again. She felt energized by the sun as it bathed her skin. She immersed herself in the strong, comforting arms of its warmth.

The sunshine offered a portal into a new life, a new life, with the promise of new beginnings. Grace started to feel that maybe this new life was going to be okay after all. Surely the dark, painful shadows from the past had gone from her life, never to return.

Even Kate had begun getting up much earlier, and was cooking breakfast in the mornings again, or at least, heating up leftover pizza from the night before. And, now and then, Asian food, now that Asian takeaway food menus had been added to the refrigerator door. But Grace didn't mind; it was still a beginning, and she welcomed any new beginnings with open arms. She still missed her breakfasts with Wade, though; Wade had made breakfast fun.

On the weekends, Kate cooked pancakes and drenched them in maple syrup and whipped cream, just the way Grace liked them. Just the way her father had liked them.

"Maple syrup from Canada," Grace informed Angela. "Dad said the Canadian maple syrup was the best in the world. Didn't he, Mum?"

"He most certainly did," Kate said, flipping a pancake in the sizzling hot fry pan. She pressed it down with an egg flip and waited for the edges to turn a perfect golden brown before she slid it from the pan and added another scoop of batter.

Grace frowned. She was thinking about her father. "Pancakes were dad's favorite. We used to have them every weekend when he was home..." She chewed her bottom lip as she thought about the last time she had eaten breakfast with her father. It felt like such a long time ago, now.

"Okay, here we go," Kate said, bringing a loaded plate of pancakes to the table. "Dig in while they're hot, folks."

She passed the bottle of maple syrup across the table to Angela. "I see your fringe has eventually grown back, Angela."

"Yes, no more, um, bad hair days," Angela responded, combing her fingers through her perfectly satiny straight fringe.

"Yes, no more bad hair days," Kate repeated, sitting down at the table.

Grace had a feeling that her mother was thinking about Brian, too, as they ate their pancakes in silence, and she knew that would never change, no matter how much time passed.

She added a spoonful of cream in the middle of her pancake and spread it out carefully to the edges with the back of her spoon. Then she drew a smiley face on it with the maple syrup—just the way her father had.

She could still feel her father's presence at the kitchen table, watching over her. Occasionally, she sensed her father's breath on the back of her neck, whispering softly to her.

"Good morning, Grace, I hope you saved some of those for me?" he would say, teasing her. He'd have ruffled her hair with his hand as he passed.

Then she would feel a fresh spasm of despair

engulf her when she spun around to discover that no one was there.

Daddy, where are you? Grace wondered, barely able to restrain the onslaught of fresh grief that tore through her heart like a razor-sharp sword.

She held her breath. She had not seen Brian, but she knew he was still there somewhere; his scent was unmistakable, the scent of *Bvlgari*, her father's favorite aftershave, hung in the air all around her. She drew in another long breath, savoring it.

Her mother walked past her, resting a hand on her shoulder. "Eat up, Grace. Before they go cold." Then she realized, with acute sadness, that it was her mother who was wearing the cologne. She imagined that her mother wore it now to remind her of her father.

So the magical bubble of new hope - that Brian was still there - popped, and he was gone again.

11 – FREAKISHLY NORMAL

Life was good, well, a lot better than it had been for Grace, all things considered.

She had made not just one friend, but two. And these two friends were not figments of her vivid imagination like Hope had been. An imagination born from her desperate need to fit in and be normal.

Other children her age, sensing that there was something different about her, had shunned Grace for most of her young life, leaving her alone and withdrawn.

She had sat with her father, anguish contorting her pretty, upturned face.

"I just want to be normal, Dad," she pleaded with her father, as though he could make it so. "Have friends like everyone else. That isn't too much to ask for, is it?"

Brian tried to comfort her. "Grace, being normal isn't always what you think it is. It isn't always a virtue. Sometimes being special is more important."

"I don't want to be special or important, Dad. I just want to be normal. I want to have friends, go to the movies, and have sleepovers, like the other kids do at school."

"We can go to the movies anytime you want, Grace. We'll all go this weekend. What do you want to go and see?" Brian asked, flipping through the newspaper to search for the movie times.

"No, Dad, it's not the same, but thanks," Grace replied, dragging herself off the kitchen chair and into her bedroom.

Hope sat on the end of the bed with her eyes closed, waiting for her. Her hair fell long and golden to her waist. Her cherub lips were blood-red and slightly parted. Grace sat down next to her and folded her hands in her lap. "Why can't you be real?" she asked wistfully. Hope opened her crystal blue eyes and wrapped an arm around Grace's hunched shoulders. "I wish I could do that for you, Grace, really I do."

"Dad says I'm special, but I don't feel special. I feel like a freak, freak, *freak!* Everyone at school just stares at me as if I've got the black plague or something. That's what being special feels like! I hate it!" she said, with tears spilling from her eyes.

"I'm sorry, Grace, but all I can tell you is that you won't always feel that way."

"It's okay, Hope," she said, wiping her tears away. It's not your fault. At least I have you, and Mum and Dad."

But the two new friends Grace had now, Angela and Joshua, were normal and real enough for Grace—

made of real flesh and blood. For once, Grace didn't feel like a loner, a freak. For once in her life, people had stopped staring, and she felt freakishly normal.

She was floating on a blissful cloud of normality. Being normal, Grace decided, really was the most exquisite feeling in the whole wide world. To hell with being special. She wished so much that her father could see how happy she was, being normal.

And to top it off, her mother was back to doing the usual motherly things. Well, Kate's version of motherly things, that was. So, yes, life was looking up for our Grace.

That was, up until the day Grace found Wade standing statue-like at the kitchen table after school one Friday.

Overjoyed with the utter delight of seeing Wade again, Grace's whole body buzzed from head to toe with electric energy. The last time she had seen him, in uniform… The smile on her face disintegrated as panic and fear ripped through her. Fear grabbed her by the neck. *Oh God, not again*, Grace thought, trying to ignore the bile burning the back of her throat. She swallowed, forcing the foul-tasting vomit back down.

A sudden thought incapacitated her. What if it was her mother who had been taken from her this time? She looked frantically around the room, searching for her mother.

Where are you, where are you, where are you? She wanted to scream out, but no words escaped from her mouth, only a screeching, rasping sound. The twisted, blackened fingers of fear squeezed her throat harder, gagging her.

Grace sucked in a breath between her teeth and held onto it until she started to feel dizzy. Her heart pounded hard in her chest. White, hazy dots began to blur her vision. *No, no, no,* she begged silently. *Yes, yes, yes*, her demons spewed back at her as they squeezed her throat tighter. *You are damned. Your soul belongs to us,'* the voices shrieked as they closed in around her shrinking body.

12 – THE ABILITY OF COERCION

Angela touched Grace lightly on the shoulder, then gave her a little shake with both hands. "It's okay, Grace. Calm down, take a breath. Breathe."

Kate stepped out from behind the open fridge door with a carton of milk. She was smiling as she went about making coffee.

Grace closed her eyes for a moment and exhaled. Thank God, she prayed quietly to herself. She heard her demons howl in defeat as they released their stronghold grip from around her throat and vaporized into thin air.

"Hi, girls," Kate said in a singsong voice as she beckoned them into the kitchen. Then she frowned. "Grace, are you okay, you look pale?"

Grace nodded mutely, forcing a smile for her mother's benefit. "I'm fine," she said, after a moment, when she realized that Wade was there as a friend and not as an officer of the law.

Kate stopped what she was doing and frowned. "You remember Wade, don't you, Grace?"

Grace smiled, then flew into Wade's outstretched arms.

"Of course," Grace said. "Where have you been? I've missed you so much."

"I've missed you too, kiddo," Wade replied, hugging Grace back, then spinning her around before setting her back down on the floor. "What's been happening, kiddo? Anything I should know about?" he asked, tousling her long fair hair.

"Tons of stuff," Grace said excitedly, beaming up

at him, elated that he was back. He *was* back, wasn't he?

She narrowed her eyes. "You're not going to disappear again, are you?"

"Nope. Not for a while."

"A while?"

"Not for a very long while."

"Are you sure about that?"

Wade nodded. "I'm pretty sure about that." He looked across at Angela. "I notice you've made a friend."

"Yes, I have," Grace announced proudly. "This is my friend Angela."

Angela approached Wade confidently, her small frame overshadowed by his tall one. She dropped her bag on the floor by his feet, and, with absolutely no apprehension put her hand out. "It is very nice to meet you, Mr Wade. My name is Angela Oaks. I am eleven years old, nearly twelve, and I reside in the house next door."

She thrust her small hand assertively into his open palm. Wade, prepared for the electric charge that would resonate through their hands as he closed his fingers gently over her tiny ones. He smiled at her neatly trimmed fingernails; each painted a different color.

The ceiling lights flickered and, with an urgent sense of danger, Angela ripped her hand from his grasp. She stared up at him questioningly with unblinking, violet eyes as large as saucers. Her tiny frame tensed. Was this man friend or foe?

"How strange," Wade said, looking up toward the light, drawing Grace's scrutiny away from Angela's response to the electrifying handshake.

A half smile formed on his lips as he looked back down into Angela's reproachful eyes. Silently, he said, *'there is no need to fear me, Angela, you know me.'* Then aloud, he said. "It's very nice to meet you, Angela Oaks, eleven years old, nearly twelve, residing in the house next door," Wade replied, mimicking her robotic tone.

Angela frowned. She still had so much to learn when it came to what would be considered a normal response for an eleven-year-old. She continued to examine Wade and responded with a quick nod and a sniff. Once satisfied with her assessment of this being, Angela stepped back again and stood protectively by Grace's side. It was wise to be cautious. The enemy had become the masters of disguise. Trust had to be earned.

'Yes, now I know who you are,' was her silent reply.

Wade smiled. *'We both want the same thing, I assure you.'*

"Angela?" Kate said as she continued to busy herself in the kitchen. "Are you coming down with a cold?"

"I do not believe so, Mrs Connors. I am not presently exhibiting any of the pertinent manifestations that suggest I have the cold virus."

All heads turned to look at Angela. All except for Grace, who was still completely distracted by the light flickering spasmodically in the ceiling overhead.

"You say the funniest things at times, Angela," Kate said, shaking her head and failing to stifle a chuckle.

"Maybe we're in for a storm?" Grace said, strolling over to the kitchen windows and drawing back the curtains to examine the sky. "There are a few clouds coming over."

"Forget the title, just call me Wade, less formal," Wade said, returning Angela's concentrated gaze.

He could hear her methodical brain ticking over, recording, learning, as the cogs clicked quickly into place.

He reached over the kitchen table, extracted a tissue from the box and pressed it into Angela's hand. A smile played gently on his lips as he watched Angela fidgeting apprehensively with the tissue she scrunched in her hand.

"Well girls," Wade said, sitting down at the table, "how was your day at school?"

Grace babbled enthusiastically. "Really, really good, Fridays are always excellent, no school for two whole days." The flickering light and the pending storm were all but forgotten as she narrated the day's events happily to Wade. Inside her chest, a cluster of butterflies danced with glee.

"We went on an outing to the abattoir, which was really disgusting. Mum, I'm thinking about being a vegetarian, like Angela, from now on."

Kate smiled. "Really?" she said.

"Yes, really, mum, and there's this boy in our class, Joshua Deneb, Josh, and he has a huge crush on Angela. I think he wants to be her boyfriend."

Grace threw her arm over Angela's delicate shoulders and pulled her close. "A boyfriend, Angela, how cool would that be, and you're only eleven."

Angela cringed at the *boyfriend* remark and squirmed out of Grace's embrace, then scowled at her. She blew her nose with the crinkly tissue, after having come to the conclusion that was its purpose.

Grace giggled at the bereft expression on Angela's face. "What? It's a huge deal if you have a boyfriend," Grace informed the utterly unimpressed Angela.

"I totally disagree," Angela retorted, staring at the tissue and shoving it in her pocket.

"Mum, can Angela sleep over tonight? We need to talk about this boyfriend stuff."

"There is nothing to talk about, so no, I don't believe we do have to talk about this boyfriend stuff," Angela said promptly.

"Oh yes, there is," Grace said adamantly, hands on her hips to express the importance of the situation.

Kate smiled and walked over to the kitchen table with a tray loaded with cake, four plates, and two coffee mugs. Grace trailed after her, waiting for her reply. "Mum?" she asked again impatiently.

"Of course, you know you are welcome here anytime, Angela. Your mum and dad working again tonight?"

"That is correct, Mrs Connors," Angela replied, drawing out a seat and taking the piece of banana cake that Kate offered her.

"You know, I really should go over and introduce myself..."

"No, you don't want to do that," Angela responded quickly. *'I will arrange a time and have my parents come to you.'*

"Why don't you have your parents come over here sometime?" Kate said as she poured boiling water into the two coffee mugs.

Angela smiled and bit into her cake.

Wade gave Angela an approving nod of his head. *'Very impressive, Angela.'*

"Okay, sure," Angela replied, as though it had been Kate's idea all along. "I will have them come over here sometime to meet you. Oh, and Mrs Connors," Angela continued. "Would you please inform Grace that eleven is much too young for a boyfriend?"

"Of course it is, Angela. You shouldn't even be thinking about such things at your age, Grace. You will have plenty of time for boyfriends when you are older. Much older," Kate said, emphasizing the last two words.

Grace frowned, picked up the carton of milk and sniffed it, making sure it hadn't turned. When she was satisfied it wasn't off, she poured two glasses of milk, added Milo and sat down beside Angela at the table.

Angela smiled with satisfaction. "Your mother is correct, Grace. Eleven is much too young to be thinking about having a boyfriend."

"Well," Grace continued, "That is because Mum is… um, well, old."

"Hang on there a moment, who are you calling old?"

"Well, no offense, Mum, but you are. You're like thirty now, right? You don't know what it's like to be young and in love, like us."

"I am *not* in love," Angela persisted. "And neither are you, by the way."

"Oh, but I will be one day, Angela, and so will you," Grace said, pretending to swoon. "Hmm, I can't wait to fall in love."

"Well I think you have a way to go, Grace," her mother said. "Now eat your cake." Kate sat down and handed Wade a plate. "I hope you like banana cake?"

"I do, very much," he said taking the plate. "One of my favorites, in fact."

Angela sat hidden behind her glass of Milo as she watched the comfortable interaction between Wade, Grace, and Kate.

"So I suppose you think I'm old, as well, Grace?" Wade asked, taking a bite of cake.

Grace scoffed. "Of course, you're older than Mum."

"Oh, but look at that, we're old enough to drink coffee," he said, holding the mug up to her.

"Yeah, whatever. Only three years to go," Grace said.

"Three years?" Kate asked.

"Before Grace is old enough to drink coffee. We made a deal a little while back that she wouldn't drink coffee until she turns fifteen."

"Good plan," Kate nodded happily in agreement, but feeling guilty, too, for her recent absence in her daughter's life. "Thank you, Wade."

Wade smiled, understanding, then added, "Looks like we're on our way to the glue factory, Kate."

"Speak for yourself," Kate laughed. "I've still got a way to go before anyone's putting me out to pasture, or turning me into glue." Then she looked at Grace and said, "And you better remember that young lady, next time you want a lift somewhere."

"Gee, Mum, I didn't say you were too old to drive and stuff, just too old to have a boyfriend."

"Well, I guess I should be pleased that I'm still allowed to drive."

Angela studied Wade. He was tall, perfectly proportioned, and as far as human appearances went, quite handsome. He appeared to be a little older than Kate, but not much. His eyes were a beautiful green, like Kate's. Oh, it was all starting to make perfect sense to her now. The pieces to the puzzle were slowly starting to fall into place; just a few missing pieces now. But they, too, would come to her—eventually.

Angela was aware of her own strength and abilities. She also knew, now, that Wade's strength and abilities far exceeded hers. The silver-colored ring that he wore hidden around his neck, one of twelve, was proof of that—but not always the case.

Wade was the one who had sent for her only months earlier, Angela knew that now, too. He was one of the chosen ring bearers and a Royal Guard. Only four others were more powerful than a Royal Guard, and they were the three remaining Royal Guardians, the fourth Royal Guardian having been slain in the war during the March equinox, over nine hundred years ago, on Altair. These three remaining Guardians were extraordinary powerful beings. Few rivaled their power or abilities.

Wade took a mouthful of coffee and told them how he had known Brian. They had worked together for a short time at the mine in the Tanami Desert before Wade had returned to the police force.

Angela's mind shifted, allowing her to see the time the two men had worked together. Brian's accident in the underground mine, she discovered, had not been an accident at all.

There had been a violent struggle, force against force. The massive stone walls of the mine, no match for the powerful clash, had eventually collapsed, crushing Brian's body, and that of one of his opponents, as thousands of tons of rocky earth tumbled down, sealing the subterranean chamber.

But then Angela's visions changed. The new enemy, the likes she had never seen before, were coming. A new age was dawning in the New World, and it was not one humanity would easily endure. Bloodthirsty humanoid bats, blizzards and snow storms that lasted for hours, days, or even months, then burning, scorching temperatures the next. Everyday luxuries reliant on electricity would cease to exist... A new Queen in her ivory tower would decide who lived and who died in her domed arena.

Angela chewed her bottom lip and swallowed hard, then glanced across the table to Wade, catching his eye.

Subjective or not, Angela's visions were horrifying, even to herself.

Wade nodded his head in response, then picked up his mug. There was nothing he could do other than to play his part. The future was out of his control. He looked across the table at Grace. The child was oblivious as to what was to come, and the part she would ultimately play in all of their futures.

Abaddon's eyes burned a murderous yellow, and his nostrils flared. He did not take bad news well. He swatted the semi-naked girl off his lap with the back of his hand, sending her to the floor. Standing, Abaddon stepped over her sprawled as though she were a lowly animal. "You failed?" he shouted angrily in disbelief, his hands clenched at his sides. "There were three of you and only one of him, and yet you still failed? You are all useless imbeciles, it appears."

The girl whimpered on the floor behind him. "Oh, for God's sake..." he groaned, giving her no more than an angry glance. "You," Abaddon said, beckoning the black-clad doorman standing statue-like at the arched entrance. "Get her out of here before I wring her goddamned scrawny neck."

The doorman bowed and dragged the sobbing girl up off the ground and out of the chamber by her arm.

"Master..." one of the men began.

"Did I say you could speak, you worthless piece of shit?" he shouted, suddenly appearing in front of the man, fingers clenched tightly around his throat, silencing him.

The second man remained silent and lowered his

head.

"I send you to do one simple task, and you come back with nothing," Abaddon roared. "Nothing!"

His other hand came up so fast that the man was oblivious when Abaddon, with one swift movement of his wrist, snapped his neck. He released his grip and let the man fall in a lifeless heap on the marble floor. His skull made a sharp cracking sound as it hit the marble floor. His black eyes, unblinking, stared up grotesquely toward his silent companion. A trickle of blood oozed out of the side of his mouth.

Abaddon turned away from the men, his long black jacket slicing through the air like a blade. To the second man, he said quite calmly, "Take your *friend* and get the hell out of here before I change my mind." He stormed back to the long, ornate table, snatched up a crystal decanter, and refilled his goblet. He took a sip, scowled, then flung the goblet into the stone fireplace. "Bring me another girl," he shouted, waking the black inked snake tattooed across his exposed chest. The serpent quivered around his body, down his left arm to his wrist where a forked tongue flickered, then hissed. Abaddon bent his head back at an impossible angle to allow a guttural roar and a flurry of evil, black vapor to spew from his mouth. His hunger for blood burned through his blackened veins.

13 - BEING HUMAN

Angela, as though sensing Abaddon's wrath across the universe, trembled. She knew that none here, on this planet, regardless of ability, was prepared for the evil that was coming. The countless loss of innocent souls - men, women, and children. The Immense knowledge, gathered over the centuries, could stand to be lost again, should they fail to beat the enemy. None could endure the powerful onslaught from the unrestrained elements of the *WAFEs* - Water, Air,

Fire, Earth – should they be forced to do battle here on Earth.

Wade turned to look at Angela once again, understanding her mounting apprehension.

Angela returned his gaze and frowned. *'When are you going to tell Kate who you are, and what really happened to Brian?'* she asked him silently.

'When the time is right; this can't be rushed. Timing is of the utmost importance, you know that' came Wade's silent reply.

Kate frowned. "More coffee, Wade?" she asked, breaking the silence that loomed over the room like a huntsman spider moving closer toward its prey.

"Sure, that would be great, thanks, Kate," Wade answered, shifting his gaze from Angela to Kate. He smiled a smile that he hoped was a convincing. His smile appeared to work on Kate. Her frown dissolved into a smile, smoothing her furrowed brow. Inwardly, the knot in her stomach tightened, but she let it go, telling herself not to be foolish. The thoughts that haunted her were just dreams, nothing more. She was a mother, a wife - no, not a wife, a widow. The frown returned.

"I wouldn't mind another piece of that cake, either," Wade added quickly.

Kate shook herself, clearing her head and ignoring the ominous voice that whispered in her ear. "Sure, help yourself. Anyone else?" Kate asked, cutting him a slice. "Actually, I think I'll have another piece myself. It is pretty good, isn't it, even if I do say so myself."

"Yeah, well done, Mum," Grace added. Anything Kate cooked from scratch, Grace knew from experience, was an enormous achievement for her mother, and quite often an enormous risk. Eating food delivered in cardboard boxes or plastic containers was usually considered a far safer option.

They sat into the afternoon, making idle conversation and eating Kate's banana cake. All seriousness temporarily left behind—but for some, not forgotten.

The small group gathered around the table portrayed a picture-perfect scenario of a normal family discussing the events of an ordinary day.

However, nothing about this group was normal or ordinary—no matter how much they wished it to be.

Only Angela looked increasingly preoccupied with the turmoil of her thoughts. No one questioned Angela about her absence from the conversation. The silence was considered normal behavior for Angela.

Often, she'd be found sitting quietly alone, reading a book, or just contemplating her thoughts, completely distracted by another time, another place—the past, the present, the future. It was often hard to tell which time zone her thoughts drifted.

Grace, who was also used to a solitary existence, was never fazed by the lingering silences that stretched out between them. Sometimes, the pair would sit for hours in complete silence; each caught up in their own thoughts. When the silence was eventually broken, usually by Grace thinking out loud, it was a silent reply that was usually forthcoming to answer Grace's questioning mind.

Angela absently nibbled at her cake. The imminent events that preoccupied her thoughts on a daily basis, she knew would soon become a terrifying reality.

Grace was briefly distracted for a moment, too. *I wish Dad were here*, she thought sadly. The smile on her face, however, remained. Kate was happy, and Grace wanted to make sure she stayed that way. And Wade was back. Surely that gave her reason enough to be happy? Didn't it?

Wade felt Grace's sorrow; he wanted so much to return her father to her, but that would be foolish. More than that, it would be incredibly dangerous, and an enormous risk to her life and the lives of others. He pushed the idea from his mind. It was most certainly not an option worth entertaining at this time.

The small continued to laugh and talk about a variety of subjects. From a job that Wade was helping Kate get, a waitress-cum-barmaid position at O'Regans Tavern, to how Wade had been called out to a break-in.

On arriving at the premises, Wade had soon discovered an old woman wedged firmly in a window. The woman had locked herself out of the house and had managed to get herself stuck in a lavatory window, trying to get back in. Mr Dipsy, her toy poodle, had gone ballistic, alerting the neighbors to the possibility of foul play.

"That was not a pretty sight," Wade said, flinging his hands dramatically in the air then covering his eyes. "Completely commando, not a scrap of underwear!"

They all laughed at Wade's entertaining translation of the event. All except Angela, who sat there completely straight-faced. She failed utterly to find any humor in the incident at all.

"Oh, how horribly embarrassing for her. What did you do then?" Kate asked with her hands over her mouth.

"Thankfully, there was a female officer, so I gladly left her there to deal with it."

Graced giggled. "Thank goodness for the police force. Because of them, we can all sleep in our beds at night knowing that we are safe from knickerless little old ladies climbing through our windows."

Angela's eyes widened at the discovery of a plausible reason to this tale. "Yes, safe, now that is very, very important!" she said enthusiastically.

Everyone turned toward Angela, completely baffled by her sudden enthusiasm for the conversation.

Aware of her under-the-microscope status, Angela picked up her glass of Milo and gulped it down. Then, with a flawlessly straight face, she burped. Her eyes opened wide in mock surprise. She quickly covered her mouth with her fingers. "Oh, pardon me!"

Everyone burst out laughing. This time, Angela joined in and laughed, too.

"Oh my God, Angela, I don't believe it. You made a joke!" Grace said, holding her stomach from laughing so hard.

Angela grinned. She was quickly learning how to fit in—how to be human. The situation, she concluded triumphantly, had been perfectly amended—for now.

14 - CRACKS BETWEEN SHADOWS

Kate made another coffee for Wade as she contemplated what to prepare for dinner. After a little deliberation, the evening ritual began.

Kate: "Chinese?"

Grace: "Yep."

Kate: "Grab the menu."

Grace plucked the menu for the Golden Eagle home delivery service off the fridge door, held in place by a magnetic calendar advertising a pizza delivery service, also regular visitors at the Connors' household.

Grace wrote down everyone's preferences.

The menu was splattered with stains from Chicken Chow Mein, Black Bean Sauce, Vegetarian Stir-Fry, and was curled up at the corners from its frequent use.

"Golden Eagle Take-Away, Tyra Chan speaking, can I take your order, please?"

"Hi, Tyra, Kate here, from Bremer Street."

"Oh hi, Mrs Connors, what can I order for you tonight?"

Kate read out the list over the phone.

"Prawn chips," Grace called out. "Don't forget the prawn chips and crispy noodles."

"I heard her. Thanks, Mrs Connors, that will be about, let me see, half an hour."

"I think the whole street heard her. Half an hour sounds perfect, Tyra. Oh, and Tyra, no meat in the fried rice, Grace has become vegetarian."

"Oh, okay. No worries, Mrs Connors. Anything

else?"

Kate shook her head. "No, I think that's it, Tyra. Oh, one more thing if you can. Extra peas in the fried rice would be great. And please say hi to your mum for me."

Tyra made a note on the order pad for extra peas in the fried rice. "Will do."

Kate hung up the phone, which is how the evening ritual usually concluded.

Grace grabbed a pile of plates, and Angela came back to the table with the cutlery.

"Anything I can do?" Wade asked as Grace and Angela darted about, setting the table.

"Nope," said Grace, sliding a plate in front of him.

Exactly half an hour later, as promised, the food arrived. "Hello, Golden Eagle take-away," an old man announced through the screen door.

Wade greeted the stooped old deliveryman at the door. The old man's leathery skin stretched gauntly over every inch of his bent, bony frame. Gold fillings sparkled when he grinned.

"Oh good, the food's arrived," Grace said, jumping off the sofa from in front of the television to help Wade with the bags of food. "I'm starving."

Angela shook her head. The expression *drama queen* that Grace quite often used was starting to make sense.

"I do believe you're being a drama queen, Grace," Angela said, feeling proud for using the expression at the appropriate time.

"Well said, Angela," Kate said, laughing at the girl sitting straight-backed at the table.

"Well, thank you, Mrs Connors," Angela beamed, bowing her head in appreciation.

Champ, the dog with the gift of super-smell, materialized on the front doorstep, yapping excitedly.

"Arr, you a funny little dog," the old man said as the pint-sized terrier circled his bowed legs and shot through the door to find a spot beside Angela. Champ had an undeniable preference for Asian cuisine.

The bags of food dangling from the old man's gnarled fingers emitted mouth-watering aromas. The aromatic scents of jasmine rice, coriander, lemon grass and ginger wafted tantalizingly into the room.

Wade dropped money into the man's cupped hand. He counted it and nodded. "Thank you, Mister, enjoy your food, okay," he said smiling before shuffling off toward his red delivery van.

Wade watched the man slide into the seat behind the steering wheel. For a few seconds, their eyes met, and the driver gave Wade an acknowledging nod. Wade returned the gesture and waited until the delivery van had pulled out of the driveway before he closed the door behind him to rejoined the others in the kitchen.

Congregated noisily around the table, they dished up portions from the plastic containers and piled the food on their plates.

"Are you sure that's enough, Angela? A sparrow eats more food than that," Kate said, settling herself down in a chair at the table.

Angela's serving consisted of a small pile of fried rice, mainly peas, her favorite, in the center of her plate. "Oh yes, Mrs Connors, this is more than adequate, thank you."

They teased each other joyfully as they fumbled with the wooden chopsticks delivered with the meal. Eventually, though, their impatience - and hunger - got the better of them, and they reached for the cutlery. Everyone except Angela went back for seconds.

Wade continued to entertain everyone by telling humorous stories about his job as they all busied themselves with kitchen chores. He didn't think it appropriate to mention the not-so-amusing aspects of his job, though, like the other kinds of evening rituals that he was encountering more frequently now. Those evening rituals slammed him hard in the chest every time they assaulted him.

Human flesh splattered on lounge room walls, ripe with maggots. The broken limbs found dumped in plastic garbage bags, limbs that had been skinned alive. Families whose bodies had been torn limb from limb and drained of blood - which presumably was for satanic rituals. Rape victims who babbled on incoherently about monsters who had drank from them and taken their souls.

"What about dead bodies?" Grace asked with a morbid fascination. "Have you ever seen any of those?"

Wade remained silent, taking a spoonful of chicken and sweet corn soup to avoid answering the question.

Angela squirmed uncomfortably in her chair and looked at Wade.

"Grace, don't be so gruesome, you'll just give yourself nightmares. Come on," Kate continued, rising from her chair. "Dishes."

The two girls washed and dried dishes as Kate cleared the table. There were no leftovers to store in the refrigerator for tomorrow, only empty containers for the trash.

Grace gave Angela a lecture about why having a boyfriend was so important.

"One. Boyfriends can hold your hand while you watch a scary movie."

"Movies aren't scary," Angela said, wiping a plate and setting it on the bench.

"Two," Grace continued, unperturbed by

Angela's response. "They can fight the kids at school who tease you."

"No one teases me," Angela retorted.

"What about those kids that teased you about your hair that time?"

"Humph, that was nothing; I can fight my own battles when I need to," Angela answered, shrugging her shoulders.

Grace continued. "Three. Boyfriends can paint your toenails for you."

"I have you for that," Angela replied.

"Okay, okay, let me think," Grace said, picking up a soapy plate from the sink. Losing her grip on the soapy plate, it slipped from her fingers.

Anticipating what was to come, Angela spun around and caught the plate inches off the floor.

"Whoa, great catch. How did you do that?" Grace asked, stunned by the swiftness of Angela's actions.

"Lucky catch, Angela," Wade said.

"Yes, lucky," Angela agreed, drying the plate and stacking it with the others on the bench.

"Hmm, anyway, where was I up to? Four, I

think? Yes, four," Grace said continuing with the dishes piled in the sink.

Angela turned her back on Grace and rolled her eyes. She should have just let the plate smash on the floor. Cleaning it up would have been far less painful than listening to another one of Grace's lectures on boyfriends.

Wade chuckled under his breath, listening to Angela's thoughts as he collected plastic containers and soft-drink bottles of the table and shoved them into garbage bags. This is what garbage bags were intended to be used for – trash - not human remains.

Wade hauled the rubbish bags outside, opened the bin and tossed them inside. It was hard to see garbage bags nowadays and not think about the ones stuffed with broken bodies. And the stench of decaying flesh, that was something that haunted him daily in his new job.

He watched as ominous dark clouds began to coagulate in the night sky. A brisk breeze scuttled through his brown hair, coercing a stray tuft to fall across his brow.

Curtains billowed in the open windows and tree branches shushed as they swished in the wind. Loose leaves fell aimlessly to the earth below. A lone dog barked, and others joined in on the raucous chorus. A silent cavalcade of flying foxes moved stealthily overhead.

Wade paused for a moment, listening, and then focused on the voices inside the house.

Grace's voice. "He does so, Angela. I know it. Can't you tell by the way he looks at you? He can't keep his eyes off you, and all that grinning, ugh. That's a sure sign Josh is love with you."

Kate's voice. "Don't tease her, Grace; you can see it makes her uncomfortable. Champ, put that shoe down, no, no, stop, stop, drop it! Oh God, look at it. Naughty boy, Champ! Grace, how many times have I told you to put your shoes away?"

Grace's voice again. "Is there any ice-cream, Mum?"

Kate. "In the freezer. Dish everyone up some, will you?"

Grace. "Can we eat it in front of the telly?"

Kate. "Sure, but not before you put your shoes away. Before Champ gets a chance to start eating the other one."

The voices reminded Wade of another time, another life, another family. His memories collided, both Brian and his. Two lives, two souls merging as one. Raking his fingers through his hair, Wade composed himself, then went back in to join this family. Brian's family. His family, Wade's family, was gone, lost to him forever. Guilt gripped his heart, and he drove the memories from his mind, they would do him no good now.

The screen door closed slowly behind him with a gentle click. Frogs croaked. Thunder grumbled.

Things that were far more threatening were on his mind, like the danger that he knew was lurking silently in the cracks between the shadows.

15 - THE THINGS YOU DON'T SEE

"We're going to my room now, Mum. Lots of girl stuff to talk about," Grace said, pulling Angela off the sofa and onto her feet.

"Do we have to?" Angela groaned.

"Yes we do, it'll be fun."

"For whom?"

Grace halted in front of Wade. "Are you sleeping on the sofa tonight?"

"We'll see."

"Please," she begged.

"You miss my bacon and eggs that much, hey?"

"Yes, I miss your cooking, but I've decided not to eat meat anymore, remember? The abattoir... I'm a vegetarian now, like Angela."

"Oh yes, of course," Wade nodded. "I had forgotten about that."

"What's wrong with my cooking?" Kate injected.

Grace stared at her mother and frowned. "Are you serious?" Then she smiled. "It's just that, well, heating up leftovers isn't really cooking, Mum... That's called nuking." Noting the look on her mother's face, she quickly added, "Your banana cake and pancakes are great, though, the best. Honestly."

"Okay, I get it. Good save, by the way. Anyway, I'm not complaining. I could do with a good sleep-in. Wade, the kitchen, and the brats are all yours in the morning."

"Sure thing, you know there aren't going to be too many sleep-ins when you start working, so you may as well make the most of it," Wade replied, kicking his shoes off and sticking his feet up on the coffee table. Grace stared at him, open-mouthed.

"Grace, what's up?" Wade asked.

Grace glanced at her mother, but Kate was too busy flicking through the channels to have noticed.

"Oh, *Abyss,* let's watch that, I love that movie," Kate said enthusiastically.

Grace snapped her mouth shut and returned her gaze to Wade.

"Oh, um, nothing... I'll see you in the morning for breakfast. Night, mum. Come on, Angela, let's go." Champ sprang off the sofa and scurried down the hall after the girls. Angela walked a few paces behind Grace. "Are you all right, Grace? You look like you've seen a ghost." Wade watched them go. "See you in the morning, kiddo, night, Angela," he said, withdrawing his feet from the table. Keeping his secret from Grace was going to be a lot harder than he had anticipated. "Night, Grace, Angela, don't stay up too late," Kate echoed, blowing both girls a kiss. "I'll come in and check on you both a little later. Have you seen this movie, "Abyss?" she asked Wade, making herself comfortable on the sofa. "Have you got a box of tissues ready?" he replied. "You know you're definitely going to need the tissues."

Grace looked over her shoulder at Angela and shook her head. "It's just something that Wade did. It reminded me of..." She shook her head again. She knew Angela wouldn't understand. Angela hadn't known her father. How he would kick off his shoes and stick his feet up on the coffee table to watch TV. "It's nothing, forget it."

Grace came to a halt outside her bedroom. She reached her hand carefully around the doorway, feeling the way until she found the light switch. She flicked it on, then sprinted over to the windows and wrenched the curtains closed.

"You truly are a worry," Angela said, strolling casually in after Grace. "Ever since you watched that ridiculous movie about the vampire with the red blinking eyes staring through the window, you've been terrified of the dark."

Angela sat herself down on the end of the bed and tucked her legs up beneath her. "I fail to understand, Grace, why you watch horror movies if all they accomplish is terrorizing you half to death. Honestly, Grace, where is the logic in that?"

Grace looked at Angela as though she'd just said something quite moronic. "Seriously, Angela. What planet are you from? That is the only reason why you watch horror movies in the first place, to frighten the crap out of you. It's fun." Grace dropped down on the bed with a grin then turned on her CD player.

Utterly dumbfounded by Grace's reasoning, Angela shook her head. "Horror movies never frighten me. They're just ridiculous fictitious stories that do nothing but discompose the brain. Nothing of importance is ever learned by watching them."

Real life, Angela thought, when things really did go bump in the night, now that was something to be genuinely concerned about. And it was the things that you didn't hear, didn't see; they were the most frightening of all.

"Yeah, well, I don't know about, decomposing the brain -"

"Discompose; it means upset, muddle," Angela

cut in.

"Whatever. I know that when a monster is chasing you, you take your high-heeled shoes off and run like the devil himself was chasing you. I've learned that... and you never, ever, dangle your legs over the edge of the bed at night, and clowns, well, they're just way too freaky, so lets not even go there. If the monster doesn't get you, the clown sure will." Grace shuddered, recalling some of her dreams about monsters and clowns.

"Are you listening to yourself, Grace?"

Grace shrugged. "Well, everything aside, they're just movies for entertainment. They're not meant to be educational or anything."

"And do you really think that closing the curtains at night is going to make any difference when it comes to keeping the monsters out?"

Grace grabbed a pile of magazines off the floor and handed Angela one.

"You're right, of course. Maybe I should lock all the windows, as well."

"I'm here, Grace. You'll be fine."

Grace let out a laugh. "To hell with that, you couldn't fight yourself out of a wet paper bag. I'm locking the windows."

"Oh, sit down, Wade is here, you'll be fine."

"So true, but still, I'll only leave the window open just a crack, just in case he's a heavy sleeper."

Angela threw her arms up in the air. "I give up," she said, returning to the magazine in her lap and flicking through the pages of glossy advertisements. "Why do you waste so much money to read advertisements?" she asked.

Grace squinted at her friend. "I don't. I pay for the articles and the fashion. "Look at this dress, it's beautiful, isn't it."

"Angela shrugged. "If you say so."

Grace's bedroom walls were a delicate, soft pink. However, that was almost impossible to tell nowadays. Only small slits of paint were visible between the gaps left by large glossy posters of Orlando Bloom, Avril Lavine, *Pink*, *Harry Potter*, *Star Wars*, and *Lord of the Rings*.

Grace sprawled out on the bed and flicked

through *Today's Teenager,* even though she wasn't quite a teenager yet.

Angela read an article on *The Tree of Life*, a book depicting the life of Charles Darwin. Darwin had written: 'At each period of growth all the growing twigs have tried to branch out on all sides, and to overtop and kill the surrounding twigs and branches, in the same manner as species and groups of species have at all times overmastered other species in the great battle for life.' "How fascinating," Angela murmured.

Grace studied a quiz on how to determine if a boy had a crush on you—or not. She devoured the column fanatically and wrote her answers down on the edge of the page. Some she deliberated on. Some she circled without hesitation. Then she added up her score.

Angela tensed herself and waited for the in-depth explanation that was sure to follow.

"Ha, ha, I knew it. Josh has got a crush on you." Grace laughed, throwing a pillow at Angela. Angela's hand sprang out and caught it. Champ sat up fiercely and retorted with a yap at Grace before resuming his sleeping position in the middle of the bed.

"Sorry, Champsie," Grace said as she patted his fluffy white head, then looked at Angela, still holding the pillow in the air. "You really are a very good catcher; maybe you should join the softball team at school."

"I don't think so," Angela said, handing the pillow back to Grace.

Grace returned to the open page of the magazine she was reading. "Now, according to this quiz, Josh is seriously into you," she said, pushing the magazine toward Angela.

Angela readjusted herself on the bed, then picked up the magazine. "Well then, I had better study this then, hadn't I? I obviously have a lot to learn, when it comes to boys."

Grace nodded. "Well, I have read tons of this stuff, so if you have any questions."

"I will be sure to come ask you."

"Good." Grace let herself flop back on the bed. "Josh really is quite good-looking, don't you think? I wish someone liked me the way he likes you."

Angela sighed. "Joshua is intelligent in his own way, I suppose."

"Who cares if he's intelligent, he's nice looking too, don't you think? A bit on the skinny side, maybe. But nice looking, right?"

Angela looked up at Grace, then to the poster on the wall behind her head. "Yes, I suppose he is, but he's not as good-looking as—" Angela scanned the poster for a name. "Orlando Bloom. We should hire *Fellowship of the Ring* this Saturday, have a movie night."

Although Angela failed to understand Grace's constant fascination with boys, she played along. Boys were an important part of the game she knew she had yet to master if she wanted to maintain a central position in Grace's life.

And the boy Josh, Angela had already realized his importance in the future. He, too, was most certainly worthy of her undivided attention, just not in the way that Grace had planned.

Angela was aware that the elements were

drawing precariously closer together, in preparation for what was to come. The fact that the boy obviously had feelings for her was just going to make Angela's task that much easier, or at least, she hoped it would.

Angela smiled at Grace, then returned her gaze to the magazine. "Yes, Josh is good-looking."

Grace crossed her legs. "Actually, a movie night is a pretty good idea, Angela. You want to know what another really good idea is?"

"Am I going to be able to stop you?" Angela inquired, turning a page.

Grace ignored her. "Maybe Josh can come over, too. He only lives two blocks away, what do you think?"

"You can't even begin to imagine what I think about that. But you aren't going to let this Josh thing go, are you?" she asked, not taking her head out of the magazine. "I'm inclined to believe, though, that it's a pity you're not this persistent at school with math. You'd be a lot better at it if you exerted just a fraction of the interest you invest in these magazines and boys." She looked up at Grace. "I'm sure you can invite Josh to movie night, it's your house, isn't it?"

Grace grinned at Angela and bounced up and down on the bed. "Let's go to his place tomorrow and ask him," she said.

Angela put down the magazine, stood up and pulled her hair up into a ponytail. "I will leave you to mastermind your grand plan for the weekend." Grabbing her pajamas from her overnight bag, Angela disappeared down the hall to the bathroom.

Grace called after her, "I don't mind if I do. Oh, and Angela?"

"Yes, Grace," came Angela's muffled reply from the bathroom.

"He really does have a crush on you, you know?"

"Oh, for the love of God," Angela muttered, closing the bathroom door behind her.

Grace made a list.

Visit Josh.

Get Wade to drive us to the shop.

Hire movie.

Buy Popcorn, Maltesers, ice cream, soft drink

Order pizza x 2—vegetarian.

"The perfect weekend," she said, rubbing Champ playfully on his head. "What do you think, Champsie? Sound like the perfect weekend to you?"

Grace could hear Angela brushing her teeth in the bathroom. She heard a current weather update on the TV in the lounge room, thunderstorms predicted for the weekend. She could hear Kate fussing in the kitchen, and chatting about starting her new job at the Tavern.

Kate was looking forward to starting work, earning the much-needed income.

"I'm worried about how much time I will be leaving Grace alone at home in the evenings."

Wade got up from the sofa and leaned against the kitchen counter. "I can call in after work, make sure she's okay, if you'd like?"

"Really, you wouldn't mind? I would be really grateful, and I know Grace adores you."

"The feeling's mutual, she's a good kid. I'm more than happy to drop in and check on her. It'll give me someone to eat dinner with."

"Thank you, Wade. Really. Thank you. You have no idea what this means to me. Not just this, but everything, the job. You've done so much for us already." She looked at him, a curious expression on her face. She had no idea why she had trusted him from the very first day he had turned up on her doorstep. He had brought her the most horrible news. He had told her Brian was dead, and now he was a regular visitor in their home like he had always been a part of their family. She wondered if Brian would have approved. Intuitively, Kate sensed that Wade had suffered a similar loss, so perhaps he needed them just as much as they needed him.

"It's okay, Kate, really. I'm more than happy to help out. It's the least I can do."

Kate smiled. Then in two steps she was pressed against him and hugging him. "Thank you so much."

He didn't return the gesture; he didn't think he would be strong enough to hold himself back, so he left his arms hanging limply by his sides like deadweights.

Kate pulled away and blushed. "I'm so sorry. I didn't mean to. I didn't mean to make you uncomfortable... I am just so... grateful," she said in a small, embarrassed whisper.

"No, I'm sorry, Kate, you just took me by surprise. Here, let me help you put these dishes away."

In her room, Grace smiled; it was the perfect Friday night, the perfect beginning to the weekend. Well, almost.

"No more school for two whole days, Champsie," Grace said.

Monday felt like a million miles away. More importantly, Grace felt happy because her mother was happy. And Wade was back. She thought about Wade for just a moment, then let her thoughts slip slowly from her mind. Silly thoughts, impossible, crazy thoughts.

She picked up her hairbrush and jumped up and down on her bed, singing along to Avril, waking Champ from his blissful sleep. He yapped excitedly, joining in, or was he angry with her for waking him again?

Sometimes, as I drift in and out of Grace's thoughts, I realize how difficult it is to separate my reality from hers, what is real for her, and what is not. It is true, masks camouflage the faces of both good and evil, keeping hidden what is a truth, and what is a lie. When I eventually reveal myself to Grace, which mask will I be wearing? I wonder.

A gentle breeze stole carefully through the open bedroom window. The curtains fluttered with the brief interruption, then fell still. A silent prophecy translated by air draws the pending storm, hovering menacingly on the distant horizon. Outside, the thorny fingers on a crimson bougainvillea scraped angrily across the glass windowpane.

Grace didn't notice the bedside lamp begin to dim, and then flicker.

Yes, it was the things you didn't hear, didn't see, lurking in the shadows at night, that you should scare you the most.

16 – BOXING DAY

Year: 2004 AD

"Tis the season to be jolly, Fa la la la la, la la la la," Grace sang as she wiped the sleep out of the corners of her eyes and swaggered into the lounge room to join Kate and Wade.

"What's for breakfast, and how did Boxing Day get its name? That's what I want to know."

"Hush for a moment, Grace," Kate said, her eyes not shifting from the images of destruction on the television screen.

Wade was sitting on the sofa beside her, elbows resting on his knees. He was wearing his boxer shorts and a t-shirt, from spending another night on the sofa.

Kate and Wade were both transfixed by the television screen, hanging off every word spoken by the young TV news reporter.

"There was no warning system in place; thousands of souls have been lost…"

"What's all this about, what's happened, what's been lost? Has Angela or Josh called yet? We're meant to be catching up at his place after breakfast," Grace asked.

She walked over to the Christmas tree to tap some of the brightly colored fairy lights. They started to blink, fast then slow, off then on.

"No. Not yet," Kate replied, still staring at the television, and shaking her head, shocked by the terrible catastrophe that was unfolding in front of her.

"I love Christmas, so pretty… Fa-la-la-la-la, la-la-la-la." Grace pushed herself up on her toes but wasn't quite tall enough to adjust the angel sitting precariously on the top. She dragged over a chair and climbed up on it. "That's better, Hope, can't have you falling off your perch, now, can we?" She jumped down. "So, does this mean I have to get my own breakfast?"

"Shh," Kate and Wade both said this time.

Then Kate said, "There are leftovers in the fridge, help yourself."

The National Nine News reporter continued with his ongoing dialogue. "Disposing of the dead to try and save the living... No one saw it coming until it was too late."

"What's too late? Grace asked, pulling the fridge door open to gaze at the vast array of leftover food from Christmas day.

She scooped up some custard on her finger and stuck it in her mouth. "Hmm... custard for breakfast." She glanced over her shoulder at her mother, then washed it down with a mouthful of water straight out of the jug.

"Shh..." Kate said, then turned the volume up. "And don't eat all the custard for breakfast. And use a glass."

Mothers, Grace decided, really did have eyes in the back of their heads.

Images of death and devastation filled the television screen.

"Officials in Indonesia, Sri Lanka and India have all reported death tolls in the thousands, and the figures are expected to rise significantly over the next few days. A UN emergency relief co-coordinator has said that this may be the worst natural disaster in recent history."

Grace stood frozen at the open fridge door; she felt her hands curl into tight fists. Her nails dug into her palms, breaking the skin. An ice-cold shiver ran up her spine. She trembled and let herself sink slowly down to the kitchen floor. She shoved the fridge door closed with her foot, rattling the contents on the shelves.

"You okay in there, Grace?" Wade called over his shoulder.

"Sure," she replied from behind the kitchen counter, out of sight. She pulled her knees up under her chin and hugged them tight against her chest.

The reporter continued.

"Other stories tell how a father in Sri Lanka watched helplessly as his entire family was swept away by the sea. Health experts are now fearing that many more could die, as diseases like typhoid, cholera, and malaria spread rapidly throughout the affected areas."

Grace tucked her head between her knees. *Oh God, oh God, oh God.* She felt herself being pulled away, back into the past. Back into Juliette's past. My past. Grace squeezed her eyes shut to drive away the ringing in her ears. Then came the deafening silence and the blinding white light. Grace was gone, and I felt the presence of another life pouring into the body Grace, and I shared.

17 – HELLS BELLS TOLL FOR THEE

Year: 1755 AD

My eyes are closed tight as I desperately try to hold on to my wavering sanity. The words of a Christmas carol swim around in my head.

Tis the season to be jolly...

I pinch my arms, hoping the pain will keep me connected to the present.

Troll the ancient Yuletide carol. Fa-la-lu-la-la,

la-la-la-la.

My mind is torn between two worlds—two parallel universes? I'm not sure. The accumulated energies from the past and the present collide head-on at a million miles per hour in my skull. A persistent struggle for existence, in the confined space, meant for one.

See the blazing Yule before us. Fa-la-la-la-la, la-la-la-la.

I can hear the shrill laughter of a child reverberate in my throat. An old man is swearing. Hens are clucking angrily in response.

My vision starts to focus and forms ghostly blobs of light and dark floating in front of me. Colors and contrasts begin to filter through into my dream, and my surroundings become more distinct, more real.

I hear feet running. Then I realize they are my feet, running weightlessly along a cobbled path. Someone rushes past me, more laughing. I feel the brush of skin on my arm. Loose strands of dark hair tickle my face as I run. I giggle. My long skirt flaps around my legs.

"Wait for me," I call out as I run. I run faster, gasping for breath, trying to catch up. I smash into the old man who is fussing over his clucking chickens.

He curses again. I don't know if he is cursing his squabbling chickens in their small timber crates or me.

Shame on him, he should know better. There is never a good reason for blasphemy on a day like today. What will God think about that? All hell will surely break loose to punish that man and his chickens.

He can curse all day long at those bickering chickens—or me, for that matter. I don't care, not today.

It is 1755, and Lisbon is preparing for one of the year's biggest religious celebrations, All Saints' Day. The city is alive with activity and preparation for this auspicious occasion.

A light breeze tousles my hair as I sprint down the cobbled path after Leon. He is so fast on his feet; I don't think I will ever catch up.

The marketplace is a hive of activity, teeming

with color, people, and livestock. All the usual festivities orchestrated for this day.

Papa always says, "If you haven't seen Lisbon, you haven't seen beauty." He is right about that. Lisbon is beautiful, especially on a day like today.

Papa is in church today, like so many others, but without Mother. She is unwell with the fever and has stayed at home, in bed. My sister Maria is taking care of her. She was a little annoyed to be missing all the festivities. And she wanted so much to attend the Holy Day Mass.

My mother told her to go, but Maria, being the saint that she is, said she couldn't possibly go while mother is in such a state.

Not me, I wanted to be outside with my brother, Leon, on this glorious day. Even the earth beneath my feet moves and vibrates with excitement as I run. Bells rejoice from every church across the land.

God is in his glory, marveling at his perfect creations on this extraordinary day.

I hold my arms out wide and spin around as I gaze up into the bright blue sky. I feel giddy with the joy of being alive. I am blessed, that is what my mother said.

"You are blessed, little one, to have such a wonderful life. We all are, now run off and have fun. Leon, take care of your sister."

My mother was right. Mother usually is. Later, I will say a prayer for her in church.

"Come on, Tareja," my brother calls. "Hurry up."

Suddenly there is a horrible noise, like an angry roll of thunder. Not from the sky, but from beneath my feet. The ground vibrates again, only more violently this time. Then nothing. But within moments it erupts again with a fierce intensity.

"Leon, Leon, something terrible is happening," I scream.

He feels it, too; I can see the terror widening his big green eyes as he runs toward me. I run into his arms, and we stand there, clutching each other, as the earth trembles all around us.

"I want Mama," I sob. "We have to find Papa, to take us home."

Then the buildings around us start to disintegrate.

Little bits at first, then whole pieces of walls come down. Our beautiful Cathedral falls, too. The House of God becomes the House of Death. Death, fear, panic - condemnation is everywhere, stalking us.

Huge cracks split open beneath my feet. The earth begins to swallow up people, buildings—Lisbon. Nothing, no one is spared.

Everyone starts running, pushing and shoving in a desperate fight for survival. I lose my grip on Leon's hand. I have lost him. He has been shoved away by the swarming crowd. I see the old man and his chickens. He is being trampled to death under the hooves of a shiny black stallion. The stallion rears up and tosses his glistening head back and forth. His wild eyes bulge in shock at his barbaric act.

The man's chickens, freed from their crates, are flapping madly around him in a panicked frenzy. Some are crushed by a stone wall as it splits in two and comes smashing down. Their round, beady eyes pop out of bloodied eye sockets and hold on by just a thread. Some are headless and run around in a panic, in a desperate search for their heads, I imagine.

Voices bellow and cry out in the escalating chaos. A massive church bell flips perilously down the narrow street, relentlessly crushing all in its path.

It reminds me of a parasol that I saw once tossed down the street by the breeze. End over end it went, cartwheeling and bouncing into the air until a dashing young man snatched it up and returned it to his blushing companion.

The bell flips, suspended above me, vibrating. Everything around me seems to stop for a second, then continues in slow motion. I want to scream, but my voice is too slow to respond. I close my eyes, crouch into a ball and fold my arms protectively around my head and knees. It won't help; I know that. It is purely a reflex reaction, but right now, that's all I've got.

I wait for the crushing impact. I feel the weight of the massive bell as it slowly comes down on my back, and I'm paralyzed with sickening fear.

Then I am free. Leon has seized my elbow, pulling me out from under it.

I hear the sound of the bell as it smashes to the

ground behind me. The cobblestones erupt from the massive impact, exploding into shards of flying missiles.

Leon keeps a tight grip on my arm as we run into the charging crowd. We run as hard and as fast as we can.

"Run," voices scream out. "Run to the harbor, away from the buildings, hurry."

If we hadn't run, if we had just stood there, we would still have been swept up, or drowned, by the swollen river of human bodies as they fled.

We cling desperately to each other when we reach the safety of the harbor. I tremble in my brother's strong arms as chaos shakes, screeches, and crashes beneath and around us.

Then the earth stops. And one by one the bells stop toiling as they too, lie broken and spent, on the ruptured earth.

Dust and smoke billow high in the sky, obscuring the sun, turning the beautiful blue sky into a deathly gray ghost. I cling desperately to Leon's slender body as tears forge a muddy stream down my face.

The gray cloud slowly disperses, exposing the once beautiful city, obscured now by the ugliness of destruction and death. Giant flames jump and lick hungrily at the heavens, like ravenous demons aroused by the suffering.

I hear cries and gasps from the living. Painful moans from the dying float aimlessly in the smoldering remains.

I worry about Mama, Papa, and Maria; what fate has befallen them? What sounds are forthcoming from their lips, if any, I wonder. My heart breaks. My legs crumble. I sob unashamedly at my brother's feet.

The crowd of people, exhausted and dirty, fall to their knees, too, and gives thanks to God.

"Oh, God, our Father and Savior, who of thy goodness has watched over us and protected us against the hatred of evil. Let us give thanks and pray."

Then an eerie hush descends, and everyone starts pointing out to sea.

A young man jumps to his feet.

"Look, even the ocean runs from death," he calls

out boastfully.

He was right; the ocean and all that sat upon it was running away, too. As if it was being sucked down a giant plughole far out at sea.

"We must go find Papa," Leon said, pulling me to my feet. We had barely escaped the clutches of hell, and now we walked hand-in-hand toward the Devil's new playground—Lisbon.

But the Devil was not done.

Within minutes, giant waves spew from the harbor. Few escape the fury of the massive waves as they surge forward, devouring the city as it lies beaten and burnt in their path.

Leon holds me tight; I hold him tighter, as the wall of water pushes, pulls and slams us into walls and bodies. I take a breath of air and salt water. I gag and throw up. A fist of water smashes my body against the side of a submerged building, then pushes me down. I feel Leon's hand slipping from mine, and I panic. I try frantically to hold on. I see the sorrow in his pleading eyes, asking me to forgive him. Forgive him for not being stronger, for letting me go. I see his lips forming my name. But only bubbles of dirty water gush from his mouth.

I search in the water, kicking and grabbing with my outstretched arms, reaching for him. But Leon is gone. Debris and a mountainous wall of seawater are propelling me further away. I fight for breath and voice. I receive neither.

My lungs are filling with dirty, salty water. I don't mean to, but I gulp in more water, eager to find oxygen—life.

Dead, broken bodies, faces frozen in terror, float grotesquely past me. I feel my soul fighting to escape the confines of my drowning body as it gulps painfully for air. I kick and struggle to hold on to every last moment of my dissipating life.

Images and memories of being a fetus in my mother's womb wash over me like a warm stream.

I see a girl, an Angel I think, with the most beautiful blue eyes. She is swimming toward me, and I know then that my time on this earth has come to an end.

I let go of my body and allow it to drift silently

207

away. It rocks to-and-fro gracefully in this watery grave. I think how peaceful I look in death. How beautiful, as my hair falls free and hovers placidly around my face. My colorful skirt billows out around me, like a flower coming into bloom. My arms are open wide, longing for a nurturing embrace.

I keep watching my body drift farther away as I float up. Up, toward the bright light that illuminates my heart, my eyes, and my soul. I am gone now, I suspect, forever from this place, this family.

But I am not alone; I see the faces of thousands of lost souls, young and old, that have also perished on this day. Immersed in a mass of glistening bubbles, as colorful as a bouquet of rainbow colored balloons held together by a long golden thread, we float away.

That day, now chronicled in the history books for eternity, would be forever remembered as the Great Lisbon Earthquake of 1755.

I can still recollect that life, that death as though it were just yesterday. Occasionally I still taste the rancid seawater as it filled my mouth, burned my lungs, and choked me to death. I still feel the weightlessness of my soul as it separated and drifted away in the rainbow of colors.

The elements - Earth, Fire, and Water - had indeed been unrestrained when they unleashed their fury on Lisbon that day.

Astonishingly, Air, the only remaining element that could have assured my survival on this day was absent.

Tomorrow, on All Souls Day, the Faithful will pray. They will pray for the dead seeking sanctification and moral perfection, prerequisites for Souls seeking entry into Heaven. They will kneel, bow their heads, and say a prayer for me, and the hundreds of others that died.

For now, I am dead, again.

18 – EDGE OF DESIRE

The Imperial City of Altair

Year: 1081 AD

Abaddon ran the palm of his hand slowly down Pandora's silky thigh. She turned on her stomach and purred as he trailed his tongue expertly along the ripples of her vertebrae.

"The spinal cord, so fragile," he murmured. "So easy to snap."

She twisted back to face him. "Why so morbid, Abaddon, are you feeling bored?" She pouted as she pulled the white satin sheet up over her divine nakedness. "Maybe you should join Cerberus. He appears to be more content spending his time fighting this—"

"Hush," Abaddon commanded, standing up suddenly, preparing to dress. Then he stood motionless for a moment. "Get dressed, get out!"

Pandora sat up and glared at him. The sheet fell into her lap and exposed her perfect breasts. A string of shimmering black pearls cascaded down her exquisite cleavage, falling just short of her ruby-encrusted navel. "Don't you dare speak to me—"

"Out, now!" he roared, picking her clothing up off the floor in a blur and flinging it at her. "Theria is back here, and no time to dress, take your garments with you, just go." He pulled her out of bed. "Go, go, go!" he bellowed.

Pandora snatched her jewelry off the bedside table. "I don't know why you are so afraid of that little bitch."

211

"Get out now, goddamn you, woman!"

It wasn't Theria, his sister, whom Abaddon feared, but the Grigorian Lord. Lord Cerberus—Pandora's husband—Abaddon's brother.

Pandora looked at him with disdain but refrained from uttering another word. Completely naked, with her arms laden with clothing, she swept defiantly from the chamber, slamming the heavy timber door loudly behind her.

Abaddon raked his fingers through his hair, then continued to dress. He was still holding his white shirt in his hand as the redhead pushed open another door and entered his chamber. "What, never heard of knocking, lost your manners during your visit to Earth?" he said, turning to face her. For a moment he froze, lost completely for words. Then a devious smile twisted up the corners of his thin lips.

Theria stood there, her hands clasped firmly on her hips to accentuate her new womanly form. "For what possible reason, Abaddon?" she said, shrugging her shoulders. "I knew you would sense my arrival. You've got the nose of a specter hound." She drifted around his chamber, scanning the bed, the floor, the logs in the fireplace crackling on the far wall. Two silver goblets of wine on the bedside table, candles. "It looks like I have interrupted an evening of pleasure, Abaddon." She picked up a woman's lacy camisole from the foot of the ornate four-poster bed and flung it at him. "Anyone I know?"

He studied her, watched her as she moved, dissecting her limb by delicate limb. His yellow eyes stopped on her firm breasts, just visible through her silky black blouse. A golden cord twisted tightly around her middle, emphasized her tiny waistline.

"My, my, haven't we grown? Not a child anymore, Theria. Does this mean that you haven't been feeding during your visit to Earth? How long has it been? I appear to have lost track of time."

Theria sauntered over to him, her eyes taking in the quivering inked snake tattooed across his chest. "Nine hundred years," she said. "Give or take." She ran her fingers up along the vibrating snake as it coiled around his muscular body. *So evil and lifelike*, she mused, *just like you.*

He smiled. Knowing Theria thought of him as evil pleased him immensely. "Time certainly does fly on Earth. It's only been-"

"A year, for you," Theria cut in, finishing the sentence for him.

He caught her hand in his as her fingers lingered on his chest. He maneuvered her hand slowly but firmly down his rippling torso. "How old are you now, my little Theria, sixteen?"

"Seventeen," she replied, snatching her hand away. "And you, of course, Abaddon, haven't aged a day."

"The advantages of staying in the Realm and being immortal my dear." He circled her. "So, seventeen. Hmm, very nice." He pushed her long red hair away from her face to expose her throat. "Sweet sixteen would have been nicer—sweeter." He kissed her tenderly below the ear. "Are you sure I can't tempt you in an evening of pleasure? Call it a late birthday gift," he said, glancing toward the unmade bed.

"A simple, 'Hello Theria, nice to see you again,'"

would be more than adequate, my brother," she said, circling his body now, running her hands across his back, down his arm. Knowing how much it would tease him, please him, arouse him. She glanced at his crotch. Yes, she could see, it aroused him. She dug her long nails into his flesh and dragged them across his chest, bringing traces of black blood to the surface of his skin.

Abaddon let out a growl of pleasure from the stinging pain of Theria's nails raking across his chest.

Theria trailed her fingertips through the warm blood, then smeared the sticky liquid slowly across her lips with her fingertips. She could feel the sensation of his pleasure vibrating through her, her body becoming eager and responsive. She touched the front of his trousers and ran a bloodied finger down the ivory buttons, then pulled back. "Hmmm, maybe another time, Abaddon, I have more important errands to take care of first. Tell me, where will I find our brother, Cerberus?"

Abaddon slapped Theria's hand away and retreated to the other side of the room in a blur. "And there it is, Cerberus, always the mighty Cerberus. I wondered how long it would take before you got around to asking that question. You have always been so predictable, sister when it comes to your weakness for Cerberus." Abaddon spat the words at her. He gripped the sleeve of his shirt, ripping the delicate fabric in his fury. Pulling the shirt from his back, Abaddon crumpled the fabric into a tight ball, held it to the torch flame on the wall, then flung the blazing ball ferociously across the room at Theia.

Catching the burning missile out of the air, Theria extinguished the flames with a single breath, then tossed the charred shirt on the floor. "Really brother, you're a tad too old to be throwing tantrums, don't you think?"

Abaddon glared at her. "Is this why you refrain from feeding, so you can 'age' for him during your visit to Earth? So that you can be a "woman" for Cerberus? Cerberus has a woman. He has Pandora. He doesn't want you, can't you get that through that thick skull of yours?"

"You say the word 'age' like it is a dirty word,

brother. However, being a child for God knows how many generations has been nothing but humiliating for me. And you will see, Abaddon. One day our brother will tire of the half-human whore. Truth be told, Cerberus has never gotten over that peasant girl from the forest."

"Oh, please, stop deluding yourself, Theria, it is beneath you. You are only embarrassing yourself by constantly throwing yourself at Cerberus' feet. To have him, what, laugh at you, yet again. And the girl you speak of, she wasn't just a peasant girl. She was a witch."

Theria shrugged. "Peasant girl or witch, it makes no difference to me, she is long gone. But tell me, brother, have I offended you? I've not seen this side of you very often. I must say, though, I find it quite amusing." Chuckling, Theria proceeded to drape herself provocatively across Abaddon's bed. Her floor-length black skirt, slit high on her thigh, exposing her long silky legs. She drew her knees slowly apart, giving him a clear view.

"I know what you're trying to do, Theria."

"I know you do," she purred, taunting him even further. "Maybe some things do change, maybe leopards - or in this case - snakes, can change their spots. And maybe our brother will desire me now as much as you always have. Does that thought threaten you, Abaddon? That Cerberus could desire me?" She twisted her hand in the gold cord from her waist and pushed it down between her thighs.

His greedy eyes drank in every part of her curvy, womanly body.

"Yes, well, you certainly haven't changed, have you, Theria? Still the little tease, lusting for just an ounce of attention from the mighty Lord Cerberus." Abaddon sprang across the room pressing Theria to the bed beneath him, pinning her hands above her head as she squirmed. "When are you going to give up on that childish fantasy and let me, the brother who does have the desire to fulfill every last one of your dirty little cravings, please you?"

Theria struggled in his grasp. "Get off me, you lecherous fu—"

"Theria. Language, please." He released his grip

on her a fraction. "Hmm, not as strong as you used to be, little one. You really should be feeding while you had the opportunity. Refraining has not only aged you, not that I'm complaining about that. You've certainly matured into a delightful creature," he said, opening her blouse to expose her ivory breasts. "However, not feeding has left you weak, and you know how much I appreciate a woman with a bit of fight left in her."

Theria jerked her knee up swiftly, but Abaddon, anticipating her intent, recoiled from her, and laughed. "Go," he said, waving her off with his hand. "Let Cerberus dismiss you again. I tire of constantly playing this cat and mouse game with you."

"Oh, please, Abaddon. Who is being delusional now? You have only ever cared for yourself." Theria pulled her blouse closed across her breasts and rose from the bed. She was not oblivious to the feelings he had stirred in her. How her nipples had hardened with the brush of his breath. "My needs, both nutritional and sexual, have been more than adequately taken care of on Earth, let me assure you."

"Oh, I doubt that," he said, shaking his head, mocking her. "Your companion, Caleb, is is that his name? That devious little shit is far too selfish to know how to please a real woman with desires as insatiable as yours, sister."

"Caleb has not been my only lover. I have taken many others since him. Hybrids, humans," she added smugly, her catlike yellow eyes mirroring his.

"Hybrids, ha, surely you jest. Since when have the half-breeds been able to satisfy your needs, Theria? I recall hearing stories about those having to clean up the messes left behind by you after your numerous hybrid escapades on Earth in the past. You play too rough for the likes of them, my dear. They are inferior. You must try to remember that they do not have our strength or our extraordinary healing powers. You are fortunate the hybrids didn't hold those little mishaps of yours against you and take revenge for their deaths." He paused. "Not that they would dare, I suppose, after having witnessed your so-called 'accidents.' And the humans, okay, I get that. Honestly, I do." He grabbed his crotch. "I can completely understand that temptation. So sweet, so fragile, so forbidden." He shook his head fondly. "Tsk, tsk, tsk. You are such a naughty girl, Theria," he said, wagging his finger. "Is it any wonder I adore you so?"

Theria smirked, and sauntered slowly toward him, taking his outstretched hand.

He pulled her to him and, for just a moment, held her body against his, breathing in her delectable scent. The human scent that lingered on her skin was still so potent. Then he backed away, tore at her blouse until it slid from her shoulders to the floor at her feet. "Now," he whispered in her ear as he scooped her up and carried her over to his bed, "Let me give you your long overdue birthday gift." He dropped her on the bed and began to unbutton his trousers. "Then I want you to tell me all about the girl, how close are you to capturing her for me."

End of Book One In The Paradox Series.

Dear reader, if you have enjoyed reading my books, a review by you would be greatly appreciated. Nothing that takes up too much of your time. Just a couple of sentences will do nicely. As an Indie author, reviews are our bread and butter. Patti Roberts.

Read an excerpt of the first chapter from Book Two in the Paradox Series below.

Paradox—Progeny Of Innocence

Grace is not a little girl anymore! As a teenager, Grace's visions have started to become more frequent, urgent, torturing her life further still. The answers she hopes to find in her visions only leaves her with one more questions. Who is Juliette?

Paradox

Hundreds of years ago, a vampiric faction of angels abandoned their mystical realm and began their dominance on Earth.

Progeny Of Innocence
Book 2
Patti Roberts

The return of Abaddon and a host of his most evil consorts, catapult the story to a whole new level of tantalizing wickedness.

DEFINITION OF PROGENY

One born of, begotten by, or derived from another; an offspring or a descendant.

1 – DELIVER US FROM EVIL

For as a lamb is brought to slaughter, so She
stands, this innocent, before the king.
Geoffrey Chaucer: Man of Law's Tale, 1386

The Imperial City Of Altair – The Royal Palace

Year: 1081 AD

The beast, nothing more than a frail lamb, lay paralyzed and trembling on the glistening silver platter. It lay there, exposed, with nothing to accompany or protect.

Abaddon tapped his foot impatiently on the stone floor. "Really? You expect me to feed on this, this pathetic animal?" he snorted, his arms folded defiantly across his chest. He stared down at the unworthy meal before him once again with mounting disdain. The glassy eye of the beast reflected the flames blazing hungrily in the massive stone fireplace. Frantically, its eyes darted to and fro in their orbits, searching Abaddon's private dining chamber in a bid to procure a swift path to freedom. Regardless of the desperate animal's resolve to escape this unsavory predicament, the scales of justice did not offer mercy. This creature surely was a lamb to the slaughter.

The young Mongol servant girl with a black-inked forehead backed slowly away from the table, her hands clasped nervously behind her back. Her satiny skin glistened in the muted glow of the blazing torches hanging on the high stone wall. Her head remained bowed in a show of fearful respect.

"Apologies, Master," she offered in response,

hoping to pacify Abaddon's mounting anger.

With a quick flick of his wrist, Abaddon flung an ornate dining chair effortlessly across the room and into the crackling fireplace. The fireplace erupted, sending embers into the room like a host of glowing fireflies.

Abaddon shook his head. "This is outrageous. This animal is a meal fitting a peasant, not nobility, and yet you still dare to place it before me! Have you forgotten who I am, girl?" Abaddon roared, his fist smashing down on the surface of the mahogany dining table, shattering a lead crystal decanter and a single goblet. The blood-red liquid, freed from its crystal constraints, made a slow passage down the deep grooves in the timber tabletop before droplets pooled on the cold floor at his booted feet.

The girl flinched. "Shall I remove the animal, Master?" she asked, then added, "Perhaps you would prefer the taste of my blood?" She pushed her long, black hair off her shoulders with trembling fingers to expose her throat and barely-covered breasts.

"Hmmm," Abaddon murmured, considering her

appealing proposal. "What is your name?" he asked, his interest stirred.

The blood vessel on her throat pulsed steadily beneath her flawless skin, summoning him closer. It was certainly a worthy offer and one he thought about now with careful consideration. He eyed her suspiciously, wondering if her generous offer could be trusted. It would not be the first time someone had tried to poison one of his kind under the ruse of a frightened servant girl.

He glanced back down at the animal before him. A fresh spasm of fear bent the animal's head back at a grotesque angle as white froth effervesced, then dripped from the beast's twisted mouth. Abaddon scowled. The girl certainly was offering him a worthier choice.

The scales tipped in the lamb's favor.

"Temulun," she answered softly, yet with the hint of pride. "My name is Temulun."

Abaddon studied her as one would a bug. "This would indeed be an honor for you, for your family, if I were to accept this offer, would it not?" he said, circling Temulun, tracing his finger slowly down her slender throat, then further, beneath the meager brown fabric. He felt her heartbeat quicken beneath his fingertips and smiled. "Lead us not into temptation, dear girl, but deliver us from evil." He murmured the words softly in her ear. "Are you evil, Temulun?" he asked, circling her tiny frame. "You know I have the ability to know if you are lying, and what I shall do to you if you are?"

"No, Master, I am not lying," she replied. "Your father honored our family once, many years ago, by taking my sister Cheren in the last Great War, when food had also become scarce. My family has been grateful for the opportunities that your father bestowed upon us. My only wish is to serve you, Master."

"Ah, yes, my father, the mighty Lord Grig, before his unfortunate journey into the afterlife. Perhaps your sister was a curse, dear Temulun? She was, after all, the last one to see my beloved father alive. Was she not?" Abaddon feigned a remorseful sigh. Bitter memories still toyed with his thoughts, burdening him with disappointment and resentment. He was acutely aware of his father's affection for his brother Cerberus, and Theria, his half-sister, leaving Abaddon as the outcast of the family. The Gods would certainly not favor him should anyone discover that it had been by his hand that his father had died.

Temulun begun to speak, "I've heard stories about your brother-"

Abaddon's hand snapped up and squeezed Temulun's mouth shut, her teeth breaking through the tender skin of her lips. "Rumors, the stupid stories of an old man, nothing more, do you hear me? "he hissed, shoving Temulun, and thoughts of another male heir to the Grigori throne viciously away. "Stories, nothing more," he said again, his eyes burning with fury.

Dealing with his brother, Cerberus, was one thing, but another, faceless rival to the throne was another matter entirely.

Temulun stumbled, her back slamming into the sharp edge of the massive dining table. A soft cry of pain escaped her lips. Biting down on her bottom lip, she willed herself not to cry.

The remaining silver goblet teetered precariously on the tabletop before crashing to the floor in a thousand glistening shards at her feet.

Temulun glanced down at her bare feet and edged away from the broken glass. "Apologies, Master. I will not make the mistake again," she said, wiping a trickle of warm blood from her lower lip.

Abaddon eyed the girl through narrowed slits. Inwardly, however, he was pleased. Pleased that others still believed the stories of the bastard son who had supposedly taken his father's life during a secret meeting. Rumors that Abaddon himself had made up based on his father's story about another boy, another heir. The truth about Abaddon's murderous deed was indeed still safe, the crime bestowed upon a faceless heir, who, should he ever come forward to claim the throne, would be found guilty and sentenced to death for murdering Lord Grig.

Abaddon grabbed Temulun's jaw, forcing her face up towards his. "Look at me," he demanded.

Temulun did as she was told, her brown eyes

fixed on Abaddon's yellow ones.

Satisfied she was telling the truth, Abaddon released her, then rubbed his hands together gleefully. "See that you don't. Otherwise, I shall find pleasure in feeding you to the hounds," he said, turning away. "Yes, yes, yes, I remember your sister only too well," Abaddon murmured. "My father was most pleased with Cheren's offering. She was a beauty, your sister, as indeed you are." He glided toward Temulun once again, then, tilting her head with his finger, he leaned forward and slowly snaked his tongue along the side of her face, tasting her. He had other plans for this girl named Temulun, he decided. "Go now," he demanded, waving her off with his hand like conductor wielding his baton. Abaddon saw himself as an astute lover. He was the master; his victim's sacrificial masterpieces, their worth only valued after death.

"And the beast, Master, shall I-"

"Leave," Abaddon barked, the tone of his voice the sound of a snapping whip. "A man still has to eat during these despairing times. Doors," he added, the look in his eyes mirroring the sharpness in his voice.

Two black-clad Mongol guards heaved the heavy timber doors open effortlessly. Their long beards, twisted and braided with ivory-colored beads made from human bones, dangled like a rope from their chins.

Temulún hesitated for a moment, then scurried quickly from the room, past the leering guards, praying that they had not overheard Abaddon's rejection of her. She would not tell her family that she had been undesired by the Master, that he had preferred the flesh of the beast to her own. She would find another opportunity, as her sister once had to complete her task. She was determined to fulfill her destiny and make her people proud.

Abaddon waited until the doors had closed behind Temulun before he returned his gaze to the trembling beast in front of him. "The things one is forced to do to survive," he muttered. He leaned forward, studying the frenzied, unblinking eyes as they watched him, then gazed further down to where the beating heart pounded against the lamb's woolen chest. "Snow white, and pure as the driven snow on the peaks of Mount An-nasr." He ran his hand down the beast's backbone, petting it, quieting it, soothing it, then he swiftly pulled his hand away and punched his fist deep into the ribcage of the animal. Twisting his hand, he effortlessly pulled the beating heart from the beast's chest. "I guess it will do." Turning the heart over in his hand, he watched it throbbing with morbid curiosity. Then, without any further hesitation, he curled his lips back and sank his teeth into the bloody flesh, savoring the tastes as one would a ripe plum. The animal's blood was warm and bittersweet on his tongue; it would suffice, ward off his appetite, for now.

However, it would not be long until his uncontrollable thirst returned, and when it did, it would not be sated by a four-legged beast. No, next time, it would be human flesh and blood he craved, and the gratification obtained from the mortal soul. The mortal soul, the forbidden fruit, the drug of preference for his kind.

Wiping his bloodied hand across his chin,

droplets of blood pockmarked the front of his white, ruffled shirt. He tilted his head back, a guttural howl bursting free from his lips. Far below, he heard others respond in kind.

It was time to leave, he decided, dropping the remainder of the heart on the floor with a plop. The animal's blood-drenched chest was still now, only flickering flames from the crackling fireplace animating the glazed-over eyeballs, stilled by death, the pink tongue dripping with crimson saliva, hung from the animal's gaping mouth.

Momentarily satisfied, Abaddon strode towards the massive timber doors and burst through them, startling the two guards standing outside.

Pandora sashayed up the arched hall toward him, eager to resume their earlier encounter - before Theria's unexpected interruption had ruined everything. *The annoying little pest,* Pandora thought to herself, her eyes averted to prevent any likelihood of Abaddon reading her thoughts. *As if Theria's transformation into a teenager could possibly change anything. Cerberus will only ever see her as an interfering little girl with a silly crush.* Pandora lifted her chin to look at Abaddon. "Abaddon, I," she began, her eyes momentarily drawn to the bloodied shirt plastered to his chest.

"Not now," he growled, cutting her off with the wave of his hand as he strode past her, his thoughts and determination motivated solely by his unyielding need for human blood. The blood of the beast had done nothing more than to quickened his craving for something more satisfying.

"Then I will," Pandora began.

"Yes, yes. Find someone else to pander to your needs. That has never been a problem for you," Abaddon said, irritated by the sound of Pandora's saccharin voice. "I am sure there's somebody else drifting aimlessly around here only too happy to fulfill your heart's desires. Your husband, perhaps? Now that would be a novelty, wouldn't it?" He smiled, amused by his stinging remarks. Abaddon began chanting as he continued on his way. "My dear beloved Father, which art now in heaven, hallowed be thy name. Thy Kingdom come, thy will be done, on earth as it is in heaven. Yes, on earth indeed," he chuckled. "Forever and ever..." Reaching the end of the hall, Abaddon descended a curving staircase five stairs at a time until he reached the bottom.

"Idiot, man-child," Pandora snorted, turning away from Abaddon. Gathering her fraying decorum, she walked swiftly toward the two men standing on either side of the massive doors and appraised them for a moment, measuring one man against the other. To the taller man, she said, "Come, I have something for you to take care of." Running his braided beard across the palm of her hand, she rolled the beads between her fingers, then, tightening her grip on his beard, she led him away like a dog on a short leash.

The end of the excerpt from book 2, Progeny of Innocence.

Dear reader, if you have enjoyed reading my books, a review by you would be greatly appreciated. Nothing that takes up too much of your time. Just a couple of sentences will do nicely. As an Indie author, reviews are our bread and butter. Patti Roberts.

Book 3 in the Paradox Series – Bound By Blood

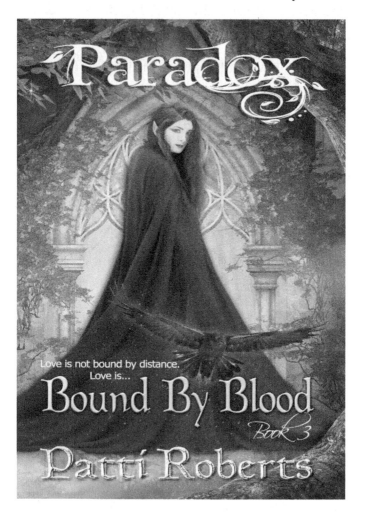

Chapters in book 1 that were inspired by and based on actual events in history

Chapter 3 Hallelujah - 7.6 magnitude earthquake hits El Salvador in 2001
Death Toll –944 Souls
http://en.wikipedia.org/wiki/2001_El_Salvador_earthquakes

Chapter 8 Kali & Bonga - Bengal Famine 1769
Death Toll –10 million Souls
http://en.wikipedia.org/wiki/Bengal_famine_of_1770

Chapter 16 Boxing Day – Boxing Day Tsunami 2004
Death toll - 230,210+ Souls
http://en.wikipedia.org/wiki/2004_Indian_Ocean_earthquake_and_tsunami

Chapter 17 Hells Bells Toll For Thee – Great Lisbon Earthquake of 1755
Death toll – Between 10,000 and 100,000 Souls
http://en.wikipedia.org/wiki/1755_Lisbon_earthquake

R.I.P

ACKNOWLEDGEMENTS

To Rory Tacchi – for breaking my heart and shoving me back on the right path. Because of you, I wrote this book and I thank you – now - from the bottom of my heart!

Every cloud has a silver lining.

I see ye visibly, and now believe
That he, the Supreme Good, to whom all things ill.
Are but as slavish officers of vengeance, Would send
a glistering guardian, if need were. To keep my life
and honor unassailed. Was I deceived, or did a sable
cloud Turn forth her silver lining on the night?
John Milton's 'Comus' (1634)

Unwavering gratitude to all my fabulous friends who have spent hours upon hours listening to me (whether they wanted to or not) tell endless stories about my fantasy family. Juliette, Grace and a world packed with an assortment of magical & mystical creatures.

You all know who you all are, and I thank you.

Trisha Dowling, Trish Thomson, Alex Thomson, Debstar Bassett, John Oxton

Natalie Hillier – for loving the book. Ella Medler for your wisdom and advice on the written word.

PARADOX — THE ANGELS ARE HERE

I would like to say a very special thanks to Tracey (Sister of the heart) and Michael (Mcgoo) who sat with me around the patio table discussing words, storylines, pizza, tequila shots and the dwindling number of bees on planet earth.

And Angela for purchasing my very first eBook. I would love to meet you one day and personally say thank you.

My sister Sue McGuinness, for taking the journey with me from start to finish. I owe you big-time for all your re-reads. Your ongoing encouragement and for loving the story – and me!

My sister Fay Maddison. Thank you for your words of support from across the vast ocean that separates.

To all my online Goodreads friends. Especially fellow Author Jayde Scott. I am grateful for your lovely words and support. Thank You.

A particular thank you goes to those of you who have bought the book. I hope you enjoyed reading 'Paradox – The Angels Are Here' as much as I have writing it.

REVIEWS

This is so totally different from anything I've read recently and I have to say... WOW. Patti Roberts is a truly remarkable writer. The way she weaves her tales among the story is extraordinary. I can honestly say I was in awe of the way she managed to do it. I'd love to have that talent. My only criticism is that I NEED to know what happens next!! I can't wait for book two!
Suzy Turner – Author

After reading dozens of Angel based books, I cannot recall a time when I said, hey - I like this. Well, surprisingly, I loved this. This book is up there on my list of favorites. First of all, the writing was excellent, I was literally flabbergasted and felt inferior in anything I've ever written.
Natalie Valdes

Are there any new Authors that have grasped your interest and why? Yes, Patti Roberts. Paradox is truly a work of art and I can't wait to read more.
Cypher Lx – Author

ABOUT THE AUTHOR

PATTI ROBERTS was born in Brisbane Australia but soon moved to Darwin in the Northern Territory. Her son Luke was born in 1980. Her son and grandson are the two leading men in Patti's life. She currently lives in Cairns, Queensland, where she is writing the Paradox Series of books. Since then, Patti has commenced writing the Witchwood Estate series, and a contemporary romance, About Three Authors – Whoever Said Love Was Easy? Patti has also published a non-fiction book, Surviving Tracy, featuring true stories from survivors of Cyclone Tracy which devastated Darwin in the Northern Territory in 1974.

Patti's books are available worldwide from, libraries, bookstores on request, and all the better online stores.

You can contact Patti direct at
pattiroberts7@gmail.com

Future books to look out for:
KLA2EEN – A sci-fi series. We are not alone in the universe.
I'm That Girl. Contemporary drama/romance.
Girl Returned – A sci-fi standalone novel about alien abduction.

In her spare time, Patti designs book covers and formats for authors.

CONTACT

Email: pattiroberts7@gmail.com
Connect with me on Facebook:
https://www.facebook.com/PattiParadox
Newsletter: http://bit.ly/PattiRobertsNewsletter

To the reader.
Find your silver lining. I did.

Patti Roberts

BOOK REVIEW FOR THE NEW WITCHWOOD ESTATE SERIES.

When you find an author with a style so perfect, so entrancing, that you know full well you'd read their shopping list if that's what they decided to publish, what could you say to make a difference? I'm supposed to be good with words, but they fail me now. So I guess I'll just have to stick to being as objective and clinical as I can. Here's what I thought of the first two books in the Witchwood Estate series.

First impression: I would read this series 'till the world came to an end. I secretly hope Patti Roberts never ever stops writing. Her imagination is unequalled.

Voice: smooth storytelling, trance-inducing, the kind that seeps into your brain and surreptitiously replaces reality with a fantastic life you couldn't help but want to be a part of.

Plot: Oh, how many possibilities! From a simple intro and clear focus, the action picks up and threads of intrigue, mystery and hidden threats begin to weave into the main fabric. As more characters are introduced, their purpose and intent are implied, understood, twisted and finally revealed to be something no one could have foreseen. There are enough twists in there for at least another ten books! And I want to read them all.

Characters: perfectly formed, from the smallest secondary role to the protagonist. Alexandria is the kind of best friend all of us need. Andrew is so sweet, and his character has so much yet-untapped potential. Then, there is black magic, and shape-shifters, and ghosts.

Descriptions: original and just right for forming the right picture. I felt as if I knew my way around, right there, in the story.

Extras: Flick through the pages, and you'll find spells Alexandria has inherited from her mother. There are illustrations accompanying the spells, with lists of ingredients, method, verses and chants to make the spells work. Patti Roberts' artistic abilities are well-known, but still, this is a very inspired little detail that adds depth and value to the story.

Emotion: The author's ability to share a character's emotion is incredible. Living as an outcast, or at least someone different, comes across *very well at the beginning of this series, and is presented with a kindness not many people are capable of. My eyes teared up because I could imagine or identify with many of the sentiments the characters were dealing with, even in this limited portion of the story.*

The overall effect is of being at one with the book. Flawless in every way, the writing is exceptional. I fell head-first into the magic and I can't wait to see where the story is heading next. A beautiful, modern tale about a witch and what it takes to make your own way in life. This is a six-star book, at the very least.

Ella Medler. Author & Editor

Made in the USA
Middletown, DE
06 January 2023